Transplanting Hope

A novel by
Jessica D. Lovett

Copyright © 2013 Jessica D. Lovett
Cover Photo © 2013 Darroll G. Wright
EMP Logo Design by ApoterraDesign.com

All rights reserved. Published in the United States by Electric Mirage Publishing.

Electric Mirage Publishing website address: www.electricmiragepublishing.com

ISBN: 1481988212
ISBN 13: 9781481988216

Library of Congress Control Number: 2013900987
CreateSpace Independent Publishing Platform
North Charleston, SC

To Trey

chapter 1

SIMON KINCADE'S SUDDEN idea about solving a plot hole in the mystery novel he was writing drowned out the heavy footsteps behind him. He was unprepared when gallons of water crashed over his weary head like a tidal wave. The icy water spilled over his back and shoulders, revving, cleansing, and making him flinch all at once. When he wiped open his eyes to the laughter of his teammates, a couple of menacing cameras were aimed at him, woven between their smiling faces.

He watched for a helpless instant as the lenses contracted to zoom in for a close up before he could summon enough power to wave them away. He heard the digital "click" sound effects, their fake shutter sound symbolizing a bygone era. Numbing coldness coursed into the neck of his cotton shirt. "You shoulda seen your face, Kincade!" someone snickered.

To this, Simon simply bowed, arms stretched out theatrically. He turned and bowed three times, making sure that all of his friends had an opportunity to get the most out of the joke they had pulled on him before he dropped it. A tall, thin man with wild curly hair threw Simon the football. He caught it one-handed.

"See ya next week?"

"Sure, Toby. Next week sounds fine."

Jessica D. Lovett

"It might rain, though, guys," a buff guy with a crew cut added, standing in the back of the crowd.

"So, what?" Simon caught his eyes.

"My wife won't let me play football in the rain," he added.

"Joe, do you have any idea how pitifully whipped that statement sounded?" Simon laughed.

"She had an uncle who got struck by lighting."

"That explains it, I guess," Simon shrugged.

"I'll call everyone if the game's cancelled," another man added as he polished his sunglasses on his shirt, "due to Joe's apparent handicap."

Simon caught a dry towel that was tossed to him. "Fine. See you all later," Simon waved to every man systematically and they all waved back. He checked the time and realized he'd better hurry if he was going to get cleaned up in time to meet George for lunch across town.

***

Bright sunlight glinted through the thick glass. Simon Kincade cut his eyes in the direction of his watch face, simultaneously turning his wrist forward and exposing the word Rolex from under his coat sleeve. Small gold cufflinks peered out also, etched with the initials S.C.K. in elaborate script. Out of sheer boredom, Simon practiced lining up one link's reflection on the framed glass of the watch as its second hand appeared to gradually decelerate.

Waiting for George in the lobby of Chemi-Life, Simon checked his watch. The clock's hands seemed to slowly decelerate. "And furthermore, the future of the company rests on the

2

completion, or the 'fixing' of this drug, if you will. Our researchers are working diligently to remedy this situation."

The balding chairman prattled on relentlessly. Simon pitied those men who actually worked here for a living, and was thankful to only be a temporary part of this dull picture. His balance on the waxed doorframe faltered. Had he just heard the word "deaths"? Surely not. Clayton must've been talking about the "breadth" of the problem or of the company or something.

The meeting screeched to a halt in tandem with the little squeak that Simon's leather jacket made against the shiny wood. All eyes turned to him. They moved eerily, almost in unison.

"In the future, would you mind keeping your guests outside the conference hall, Dr. Morris?" the chairman barked across the polished oak table, implying that Simon's peering into the meeting was annoying him. Simon thought the chairman looked like a hungry vulture as he gawked at the workers from his high perch on the podium.

The room was blank. No movement. Everyone seemed embarrassed by the interruption. A quick, insincere "yessir" slithered from George Morris's lips, ending the vacant pause in the meeting. This succeeded in making George look, to Simon, like a little kid on the back row in class caught red-handed passing a note to the next desk over. Simon half expected Chairman Clayton to dismiss George to the principal's office.

Clayton stomped over and shut the door. All sound was drowned out with the wooden door, no windows. Simon felt the Braille letters under the plaque beside the door that read "Conference Hall."

Why would Clayton think George's old college buddy cared about the business of the Chemi-Life Corporation? He cared nothing for man-made chemicals and the uses thereof.

Simon shied away from meds and tried to keep things as natural and green as possible. His housekeeper was forever getting mad at him for buying organic cleaners that she said weren't as good as the "hard" stuff.

It's not as if he hadn't seen Simon hanging around George's office before. Clayton might remember that Simon's work involves being a sort-of... well... paparazzi. That didn't look good. Yet, Simon and George had gone to lunch many times, passing by Clayton's glassed-in fortress of an office each time as Clayton averted his stern eyes. Avoiding the hassle of having to wave and fake-smile, Simon assumed. Simon didn't know why Clayton got so upset. It's not as if they were meeting about something of top-secret importance.

Still, Simon's ears burned red as he stuck his hands deep into his pockets. One glance from George told him that he'd better back out this time. The waiting room was bland and colorless, not at all tempting to a mystery writer's palate. *An aspiring mystery writer, that is.* He wished that they were meeting about something confidential and colorful. It'd at least give him a bit of fodder for his plotline, if he changed the names and detail appropriately.

Currently, Simon was doing well for himself as a freelance entertainment reporter. He had always had a certain knack for being at the right place at the right time. Gossip hungry magazines ate up his sightings of A-listers. Sometimes he felt a little guilty about his source of income, and yet what harm did it really do? And, sometimes colleagues picked on him for his choice of career, but, honestly, he enjoyed it. It's not as if he was a spineless paparazzi stealing shots of someone's child playing in the backyard. When he spotted them, they were already in public.

He didn't go out with a star map in his pocket. He got to meet lots of interesting, artistic people. Celebrities didn't run from him because of his history of writing generally flattering articles. He preferred not to use cameras; his subjects were only seen through the colorful lens of his words. They had to have publicity, right?

Besides, Simon felt that celebrities desired to be seen. He was, in a sense, helping them further advance their careers. He put their names in the hands and on the minds of millions of subscribers, not to mention those who threw the mags in their shopping baskets on a whim while waiting in slow checkout lines out of a slight curiosity that peaked at that vulnerable moment.

Movement outside the sprawling window caught his wavering attention. He sauntered over to it, eager to find entertainment beyond the limited spread of outdated, generic glossies. Three-month-old articles about the stock market condition seemed to parade across each mundane cover. Who reads this stuff anyway? The second hand on his Rolex was not going any faster. George had told him that the company's bi-weekly staff meetings usually did not go past an hour, hour and a half at the most. It was approaching two and a quarter. Simon's stomach growled on relentlessly. Don't those bigwigs have better things to do besides corral their underpaid staff around a personal soapbox? Send out a memo next time.

Poor George. A few weeks ago at their usual table in the front right corner of The Bistro, George had confided his yearning for a perfectly tailored suit. His off-the-rack just would not allow him to feel as successful as he longed to be. It had been so many years since George was genuinely proud of something he was solely responsible for. Someone else always took the credit

and he was too kind-hearted to argue. He shared the spotlight willingly.

Besides that, Simon knew that George wanted and desperately needed to vent his emotions about Emily again. He just didn't want to hear about it anymore, but George's wellspring of sorrow was never exhausted. At least, though the conversations got annoying after a while, Simon was beginning to feel needed. George had always been the foundation, the shoulders that Simon stood on.

George and Emily's marriage had gone – or had always been, in Simon's eyes – sour and it seemed to Simon as if it were just now dawning on George... what with the blatant discharge of the love, care, and affection George kept selflessly flinging her way.

Simon used to think that George was just a pushover, but that wasn't it. A example of this would be how George and Emily acquired their family pet. George loved cats, but his wife loved dogs. Yet, it was George, not Emily, who purchased the champagne-colored, perpetually barking fireball that ruled their first apartment together. That's just the kind of person he was. He would honestly rather make someone else happy than be happy himself. Simon had come to the conclusion that there was nothing concrete that George wanted for himself.

It had taken Simon a while after getting to know George back in college to realize this. At first, George's overpowering concern for others had come across to Simon as weakness, but now - Simon saw it as something he strove to imitate because he felt that George's selflessness highlighted his own weaknesses. Admittedly, Simon tended to see other people's happiness second to his own unless he purposefully stepped back and placed them in front of himself. George did this by second nature. George

was really a rare kind of guy and Simon was honored to be friends with him, though sometimes Simon wondered why George put up with him all these years. It seems like Simon was the one always getting them into scrapes in college. Not big scrapes, but big enough to ensconce in their memories as fun times, looking at them in retrospect.

At Christmas last year, Simon had resorted to buying one of those gourmet food baskets after months of futile shopping around for an object that said "Dr. George Morris" all over it. Unfortunately, he'd placed it in a corner of the dining room that he never used and had forgotten all about it until he noticed a buzzing noise. Fruit flies – how they got in his apartment, he had no idea – had found a tiny hole in the shrink wrap and were busily warring over the fuzzy black spots pushing themselves up on the clear plastic. No fruit was recognizable, all melded into a single unit of gray fur. George didn't seem to mind too much. He had lightheartedly razzed Simon about it as they rummaged for any salvageable packages of crackers and cheese during a game they were watching together a couple of days later.

George knew Simon too well to be hurt about it. He had understood the thought behind the gesture, at least. They had been best friends for ages, and Simon wasn't even sure if George had a favorite color. Emily loved anything pink, that much he knew. He couldn't help but know that, the way she carried on whenever he saw her.

Simon remembered sinking a little lower in his chair that rainy afternoon at George's confession of wishing for more concrete evidence that he was a success at engineering, causing Simon to tuck his prized watch into his custom-made sleeve. Maybe George couldn't tell that much just by looking at the part

of his sleeve exposed from inside his tweed jacket. It wasn't as if he hadn't seen Simon's watch before either.

He mused about that moment and wondered what he thought he was hiding from anyway. It wasn't his fault he had it easier than most people. As a child, his parents had left him a goodly inheritance in a trust fund, which admittedly lifted quite a few worries but did not give him a license to extravagance. Simon worked for a living just like anyone; he just did most of his freelance work at home. After all, the watch had been a gift from his mentor when his first piece was published. He treasured its inscription. The wording was an inside joke between the two men, and it always forced him to crack a smile. Simon missed Dr. Jenkins, at least three books consistently riding under his arm.

Finally, a line of gray and black suits began to trickle out of the conference room. Each face was harrowed. Simon guessed he must not have been the only one who thought the meeting was the very definition of boredom. How could they bear this twice a week? They looked as if they had all been unplugged, with all signs of energy and life spun out of their souls. So this is what is was like to have a "real" job. Simon took one last sweep out the window. The glass looked almost nonexistent. "Gray and black sedans for the gray and black suits," he mused to himself. Not one red convertible in the lot. His relatively conservative white two-door stuck out like a sore thumb.

"Simon, you fiend! You've eavesdropped on company secrets...now we're gonna have to kill ya." George chuckled at his own joke as he took hold of Simon's shoulder. "Whoa! Been working out, eh? That's not like you."

Simon had gotten a gym membership last month, but he didn't think any changes to his physique had begun to show yet.

George always noticed everything. Simon appreciated his sideways encouragement.

Lunch had been pleasant but uncommonly brisk. Somehow their conversation did not veer to anything more pressing than the weather or Simon's latest article. Simon felt like George was trying to suppress his marital woes from Simon on purpose, to give him a respite, maybe. The sunlight hit them as they ventured out of Chemi-Life's large office building and onto the sidewalk.

"How were Toby and the guys?" George asked.

"Fine. They missed you. How can they make you work on Saturday?"

"Well, some important stuff has come up. We didn't have a choice but to touch base about a few things today."

Their lunch ended as slowly as it had begun, with each topic drawn out to its full potential. They had known each other long enough to not feel the need to force idle chitchat in order to spend time together, but neither had wanted to eat in silence. It bothered Simon that they had come to have so many marriage counseling conferences that they had forgotten how to just talk about normal things. After covering his half of the check, George trotted back to the grindstone, slick briefcase swinging by his side.

With his matching ensemble, he looked more like an overzealous intern than the senior executive that he was. Simon laughed to himself, remembering the George he knew as a shambling freshman in their good old days. It was hard to believe that this stuffed shirt had once picketed down the streets for one of their life altering causes of the moment, sporting a Led Zeppelin tee shirt. Habitually, Simon looked down to check the time. The second hand was at last back to normal.

The taxi ride home had become such a mindless routine that Simon was numb to the faces of the drivers. He couldn't recall any distinguishing features two minutes after paying the fare and leaving a tip. Lately he had gotten good at guessing the exact charge without checking the meter.

Avoiding a river running down the high old-fashioned curb, he skimmed the damp sidewalk. When did it rain? How could he have missed it? He rationalized that he was too preoccupied and too tired to blame himself for not noticing something so trivial. Good thing he was finally home. Going to George's building had a tendency to exhaust him. There were so many people bustling around him that it brought back the familiar and hated feeling that he was just one more obstacle in their day, blocking their way to pressing engagements. Simon swallowed three steps with each exaggerated stride up to the jovial doorman. What a job, having to smile at people who live in a place you can't afford to live in yourself.

"Good afternoon, sir."

"Where's Reilly?"

"Day off, sir."

"Oh. Nice to meet you, then, ah..."

"Edmund, sir."

"Edmund. And I'm Simon. No 'sir' needed, thanks."

"Thank you, si...err, Mr. Simon."

chapter 2

EDMUND HOPKINS DID not know why he told Simon Kincade that Reilly, the real doorman, had the day off. That compact answer had just rolled off his tongue. Well, in a way it certainly was true. Being fired is one way to have a day off, wasn't it? The guilt still pawed at him, though. It had been Edmund who introduced Reilly to the notion of moonlighting - and reported Reilly's infidelity to the manager. Nevertheless, it could not be helped. Maybe Reilly got to keep that other job. After all, it did pay a tad more than this one. He had seen to that.

The apartment Edmund kept in this building was fine, and the strong walls allowed him to indulge in moderately loud operatic arias on his stereo without bothering the other tenants. At least, he hadn't had any complaints. His first day on the job had been especially nerve-wracking. It was awkward to be introduced to Simon Kincade since Edmund felt as if they already knew one another. Edmund knew that Dr. George Morris would show his face sooner or later this week.

***

Simon pushed the power button on his laptop. The whirring broke the silence of his darkened space. Bookshelves lined at least one wall in each room and filled every flat surface. He definitely had eclectic tastes in literature. Though he was indeed bookish, his collection would no doubt send an orderly librarian into hysterics. There was a deliberate order as with the rest of his life, but only he understood its structure. An outsider might find it chaotic to sandwich Laurence Hope's poetry between *The Art of War* and a Louis L'Amour paperback.

But Simon's system made it possible for him to find what he needed when he needed it. As a birthday surprise a few years ago, a former girlfriend resolved to "help tidy up the place." Needless to say, it did not go over well. He had this kind of problem with women as long as he could remember. They were always trying to "fix" him. He was not broken, and he only worked to sustain a relationship as long as she felt the same way. When she decided to improve him as she saw fit, it instantaneously killed his passion and he would simply let its lifeblood drain out until the relationship naturally died off.

A true bibliophile, Simon bought more books whether he had read the ones he acquired last week or not. Being surrounded by unread titles did not quell his desire in the least. Delicately unfastening his watch and nesting it face up on the desk, between a few stray paperclips and some writing tools, Simon commenced his work. Every hour he could spare was dedicated to his dream, the yet untitled mystery novel that would soon revolutionize its genre. He was sure of it. Most of the time.

All at once, incessant beeping shook him awake. Having fallen asleep with the first two fingers of his right hand pressing the keyboard, he had created a sprawling sea of the letters B, N, and M. The box in the shaded scroll bar had shrunk so thin with the weight of page after virtual page that he almost gave up and pushed the little red "x" in the top corner of his screen without bothering to save. Then he remembered what he had been writing.

***

George habitually winked at his secretary. Agnes Bloom was nearing sixty-five, but she was by far the best secretary he had ever had. George shuddered at the thought of ever losing her. He knew that she'd want to retire someday, but he hoped that it wasn't soon.

George closed his heavy office door with an equally heavy sigh that deactivated his forged smile. The smile to throw Agnes off the trail of worrying over him. Leaning against it to regain his lost composure, he took into account the fact that he had better start producing footsteps onto the newly buffed hardwood floor or Agnes would wonder over his delay.

All the home trouble and now this Chemi-Life stuff, George sighed. The issues discussed in the meeting were still preying on his mind. It seemed to him that this all started happening when the company started doing too much. Meddling in the lucrative world of pharmaceutical advertising instead of sticking to basic chemical engineering and food production. Advertising their own wares and not having someone else do it for them. Who had come up with that brilliant idea, anyway?

Agnes was a sweet lady, but she did have a habit of prying into his personal life a bit. Sometimes it seemed that Agnes worried about him too much, though not enough to make him feel too claustrophobic. It wasn't her style to nag. In spite of that, she would drop little hints here and there, writing him notes and sticking them to his desk telephone. Sometimes he grew tired of seeing those little off-yellow squares, but he knew each one, deep down said "I care" underneath its surface neatly scrawled message.

True, this kept him generally on top of things. Especially now, since all he could seem to concentrate on was Emily. He could not put his finger on what exactly went wrong between them, or when it started to become that way.

George couldn't decide whether Agnes's treatment of him was more like that of a wife or a mother. Maybe Agnes had a touch of both. George didn't know much about her family except that her situation must not be ideal. On her birthday, his were the only flowers brightening up her desk. It seemed to him that she had a richness of spirit that was too often taken for granted, making her work harder than most to please. If Agnes had been giving fifty percent of her efforts, it would still be twice that of most of the past secretaries George had been harnessed with. All they seemed to be good at was painting their claw-like fingernails obnoxious colors that clashed with their outfits so badly that even he took notice of it.

Having Agnes around made him feel secure and taken care of. No one else did that for him anymore. Her golden intentions forced him to overlook it when too much sugar occasionally settled in the bottom of his coffee mug. At least Agnes wasn't an advocate of any of that nasty fake sweetener stuff in pastel packets like his last secretary. Emily made him feel like the uptight babysitter when she was in one of her famous moods. She needed flattery and gifts at ample intervals in order to feel loved. It hurt George that Emily could not be content with unadorned words of love. His words needed to be reinforced by gifts, elevated to meet her lofty standards. George unlocked the middle drawer of his desk and drew out several envelopes with his home address partly covered by yellow post office forwarding labels stamped with the address of the Chemi-Life Corporation.

Bills. So many of them. He had begun forwarding mail to the office so that Emily wouldn't snoop. Not that he was doing anything especially secretive. He just didn't want her to know about the financial bind they were in. He wanted her to be happy and shopping made her happy. If he couldn't personally make her happy, at least he could provide the means for it and vicariously cause her momentary happiness - however superficial it may be. And even if he didn't get to share it.

Agnes pried open the door with a look that said, "Busy?"

"Come on in."

"Coffee, George. Pipin' hot!"

George didn't like his coffee "pipin' hot" but he did like the cheery way that Agnes said it so he never bothered mentioning it to her.

"Great. Thank you."

Agnes's locket swung forward on its chain as she plunked the coffee on his desk coaster. George had seen Agnes's late husband's face in the locket so many times. Agnes had often compared him to James Bloom, about which George was very flattered since he knew how much honor she bestowed upon James's memory. George wished that someone would love him – love the sight of his face – enough to put it in their locket, close to their heart.

She started, dutifully, to leave, but George felt lonely. He wanted to keep her in the room talking for a while longer.

"Agnes... so where do those cute blond grandkids live, again?"

He could see their faces clearly, beaming up at him, having walked past Agnes's desk every single day, that same picture freezing them in time… keeping them from aging. George couldn't help but notice that their mother, Agnes's daughter, was cute and blond, too. He had often been curious why their dad wasn't in the photo with them, but didn't want to ask Agnes about it. It was none of his business.

"Michigan. Jackson, Michigan."

"Pretty far away…"

"Well…," Agnes sighed, "Maybe if I had been a better mother, I'd have the chance to be a better grandmother."

"If you were as good a mother as you are a secretary, I'm sure you were the best…."

"Awww… George Morris, don't be a cad!"

"I mean it! I never miss an appointment, an important call or…."

"You'd never miss a meeting, anyway, George. Stop your flattery."

"Yes, ma'am," he teased.

Agnes began, once again, to leave. George stopped her.

"And, Agnes, please order those pink roses for Emily for our anniversary next week. I want plenty of time so they can order those perfect, big ones that they did last time. I'll write you a note to put in it."

"Of course. I'll call them right now."

***

Simon had gone to bed around eleven and had fallen asleep watching David Letterman and Jay Leno, switching channels between them during advertisements. He slowly realized that he had begun dreaming in animation. Overtly ecstatic voices infiltrated his thoughts, singing and chanting numbers and the alphabet. Simon eased open one heavy eyelid to a reception of psychedelic colors and huge smiles shouting out of the artificial darkness created by his black out shades.

He attempted to focus on the clock. It was getting to be late, and Simon figured he had better start working. Reaching through the folds of his blankets, he found the remote down by his knees and felt victorious as he eradicated the offending parade of noise and lights. Too tired to fight with the laptop, he reached into the darkness and grabbed a legal pad from his bedside table drawer.

In harmony with the rest of his apartment, books were on top, beside, and below the small minimalist table. Amid a few popular paperbacks of the moment was his digital alarm clock, framed in wood to cancel out the blatant utilitarian vibe and serving as an anchor to an assortment of pens and pencils. Still clutching the legal pad, Simon had just started to drift back to sleep when out of the stillness he heard a key scratching around the front door. It was a new brass lock and it annoyed him that she had not taken the hint, determined to scuff it up royally. Yet, she was worth the sacrifice. Her footsteps down the hall made him smile involuntarily.

"Simon! Hey, Simon!" His bedroom door opened cautiously. "You up and about yet? All this lazy...why do I bother with your lazy bones? You decent?"

"Yeah," Simon croaked. A cheerful figure danced into his room, instantly adding color to her silhouette as she proceeded to roll every window shade up as high as it could go.

"Ah! Yolanda! Warn a person next time."

Simon shielded his eyes with the navy comforter bundled around him.

"Good morning to you too," he muffled from under his tent of darkness.

"Yes, yes. Good morning to people still in bed."

"I'm working, see?" he protested, waving the legal pad like a white flag.

"Hmmm. No, this...this is work." Yolanda Ortega indicated his living environment with evident mock distain. "¡Qué lío! This place looks like a disaster area. You clean your own place sometime, eh?"

"But, you do it so much better than me, though, Yo."

Yolanda laughed and muttered in Spanish, whipping her hair into a spontaneous chignon with a stray pencil from one of his stashes as she started to the kitchen to make cappuccinos. Simon found that regular coffee had lost its appeal since he had brought home that expensive machine. He liked extra froth on his. She poured it on, and sprinkled cinnamon on top just to be festive.

"What would you do without me? Every week it looks like I've been gone a month!"

"At least I give you full credit!" Simon joked, taking his cappuccino. "Cinnamon - smells good. Thanks."

The sounds of multitasking machinery began to fill the house. Simon felt even more lazy as Yolanda whisked in a load of towels and rotated the dial to heavy duty, adding extra soap and fabric softener. Then she started the dishwasher the same way. Simon noticed that the writing was starting to come off of the "extra high" button settings of both machines, but the low and delicate setting looked new and untouched.

Extra high was her way – extra hot water, extra scrubbing, extra bubbles. Yolanda chuckled at Simon's polite attempt to load the dishes. The night before, Simon had squeezed salad bowls between dinner plates and put big grimy pots on the top shelf. She looked at him with a will-you-never-learn expression, making Simon shrug innocently. "Hey, I tried." After sorting them out, she added soap to his meager donation to the dispenser.

Simon had gotten a new flat broom that he wanted her to figure out how to use. He had bought the matching flat mop, too. He thought that they were kind of neat. He felt domestic having bought them.

"Surely you don't think that this skinny paper towel can clean up all the messes that you're capable of, Simon Kincade!" Alarmed, she checked the pantry. "Whew, that was close." The real broom, mop, and bucket were still safely nestled in their respective places.

"Thank goodness!" she accidentally let out, a little too loudly.

***

"Will there be anything else, Mrs. Morris?" the pert salesperson asked apprehensively. Emily, pointy nose thrust into the air, looked down at him through her invisible line bifocals. She would die if George knew how much her prescription had been increased over these past few years. These were the sleekest glasses that money could buy, so she didn't feel too frumpy.

Actually, Emily felt kind of brainy in them. Sometimes she was in the mood for that. Some people even found braininess seductive, journalists and writers and bookish people like that, and that fact perked up her swollen ego even more. Her eyes were red from lack of sleep the night before, from too much television, and she didn't feel like wearing her irritating contacts. George thought she was watching a soap marathon, and she had been, but after surfing around a bit, she got caught up watching a few shows centering on the ever-expanding realm of Internet crimes. One particular case had caught her imagination, one about a cunning criminal still eluding the police. The man had stolen many identities on the Internet and routed money into carefully buried bank accounts in a range of small North Carolina towns. The guy was a genius.

"As a matter of fact, young man," she turned over the prospect, "yes. I want all of this gift-wrapped. In pink, I think."

"Yes ma'am," the salesperson replied without hesitation, though his eyebrows were raised. Emily had shopped until the spectacle she had chosen earlier was enveloped in light pink paper, with wire edged ribbons of a darker shade swirling down the sides like stretched out ribbon candy.

"And have it delivered to the address on file, promptly at four. Except for," Emily drug from the pile a baby blue fuzzy sweater with tiny iridescent rhinestones around the collar, "this one. Send it to this London address, to Marlena Jarvis with a cute note that says 'Love, Mom.'"

"Ma'am, that will be an extensive amount of shipping cost and…"

"Ship it, whatever the cost. I'm familiar. Thanks."

Emily sauntered out of the store and walked into the next without thinking. Stepping inside, she was assaulted with the pungent mix of smells – all the store's lot of bubble bath, lotion, candle, and potpourri scents all mashed into one giant heavy smell. Oranges, berries, cedar woodsy scents, jasmine, rose… all the usual scents. Grabbing the first tester she saw, Emily commenced to spray on body spray and furiously rub in lotion, all in a raspberry smell. Maybe more of one smell would take away the all swirling ones around her, she reasoned.

Didn't help. She stepped outside and took a big cleansing breath. The next store was a bookstore. No bothering with that. The next an electronics store. Nothing exciting to her. She was tired anyway, so, on to the car. Rounding the bend, looking for her vehicle, she saw a blue pickup truck. Uncommon kind of car, really, but one exactly like -

Eddie Joe's. There was not a day that Emily did not lament over her beloved Eddie Joe. Shopping, sex, and other silly addictions kept the "missing Eddie Joe" part of her mind occupied enough – at least by temporarily putting other things in the forefront. Shopping gave Emily a high. A feeling that she could be whoever she wanted to be, changing whenever she wished, and distancing herself from the simple girl who grew up with Eddie Joe.

Hurting George wasn't her original intention, really, it just always seemed to happen anyway, so she had stopped trying to protect his feelings as much as she used to. Emily had stopped seeing her quick flings as cheating on George anymore – after all, cheating was taking away something from someone that was rightfully theirs. And she gave George plenty. He just didn't give her enough of what she needed, she reasoned. She required supplements to her life to fill in the gaps – more like vitamins than full-on meal replacement shakes.

Poor George still believed her, of course. She could never tell George about Eddie Joe. The lie had long since let its roots get so thick and mired that it was beginning to hold up their marriage. Emily knew that if she told the truth, that would be the end of it. Even if she and George didn't have a lot of a relationship, at least they had something. A home together. That was something.

chapter 3

GEORGE STILL BELIEVED that Emily had lost her parents in a car crash before college, just as he had. That was one commonality that George felt with Emily, she thought, having both experienced the grief of unexpectedly losing both of their parents at once. The lie was so old that sometimes Emily forgot it even was one.

She hated the person that she had become because of it, and yet her brimming indifference was her fuel, her power, helping her to step over the troublesome carnage of her past without looking back. Emily looked at her phone as it vibrated and sang a short tone in her patent leather purse. One missed call from a contact labeled "Cindy Jarvis." She clicked the dial button with the end of her fingernail, her nails being too long to touch it with her naked fingertips, and waited a moment.

"Hey, baby! How's my little girl doin'?"

***

"George, thanks, really, but..."

"But, what? It's perfect," George cooed into Simon's cordless. Fumbling around the kitchen table for his entertainment system remote, Simon asked George to hold on a minute. The boomingly loud melodic rock subsided.

"Okay. That's better. And what's the matter with the job I have?"

"What job?" George retorted. George had caught him in his tracks. The snappy comeback Simon had stored up became obsolete. After an awkward pause, he tried again. George wasn't trying to be insulting after all.

"Ah, come on. It's not that bad. Did you read my piece on the award winning Beatrice Ripley? When she was in Candelabra with her entourage? I even got the waiter to tell me what she ordered. It did take some expert coaxing, and I must say that..."

"Give me a break, Simon. You know very well you're sick of it. With this, you'll get free copies of the books you review. Autographed! First editions!"

"Wait..." Simon interrupted.

"What? You know you love books and..."

"Book reviewer copies are usually not very pretty... just the manuscript with a bare binding that says 'Review only' or 'Not for resale,' always unedited proofs, right from the publisher, not the author and..."

"Fine. Well, maybe if the author liked your review they'd send you one personally as a thank you!"

"Perhaps. But, it'll probably pay less."

"You have you dad's inheritance fund, remember, Simon. Is it suffering?"

"No."

"Well, then think of it. You'll be – almost – a respectable member of New York society. At least to those you haven't scared away with the power of your pen yet," George said, giggling like a schoolboy at his own perceived wit. Simon couldn't help but laugh with him, even though he didn't think it was very funny.

"I admit it, you've piqued my interest. You're a good sales-man, George."

"So you'll give it a try?"

"Oh, alright."

"Don't forget, Simon, you owe me for this. And to think you once doubted my vast array of contacts."

Simon put down the phone, tired from the heavy conversa-tion. He didn't want to change jobs, but George was right. He did need to stir things up a bit in his life.

Maybe since he can't change his own life, he feels like a Good Sa-maritan changing mine, Simon thought to himself as he raised the volume on his stereo back up to its original level.

***

George had barely hung up the phone when Emily clicked into the room in her loud high heels, Darby's fluff burying her arm up to the elbow. "My soap's at an ad," she said matter-of-factly. "Who was on the phone? Simon?"

"Yes," he leaked out, like a dying balloon. George picked up his Dickens hardback on the counter top, and started out of the stale room.

"I thought so. You had your talking-to-Simon-voice. Wha'cha reading?"

"Oh, nothing. Thanks for expressing a caring thought about my interests," George volunteered. *I guess I do have Simon phone voice,* George thought, surprised that she noticed such de-tails. From a place inside him that didn't feel guilty about being vaguely rude to his wife, George spoke this with tinge of mocking sarcasm. Emily didn't seem to catch it, judging from her expression, so George decided to suppress his urges and go ahead and let the sentence look unassuming.

She grabbed up the book and squinted when she saw the tiny font size, moving the text closer and then farther away from herself, as many words as possible squeezed into each page. If he didn't know that they were both about a decade off from such things, George thought to himself, he'd think that his wife needed reading glasses.

"No problem. I was just trying to make conversation and all," Emily said as she flipped her ponytail and waltzed out first, beating him again.

Straightening his tie, George counted to ten as he inhaled and exhaled deeply, biting his tongue progressively harder. Emily always needed to be first in line, first to leave, and the first to initiate a conversation. He was determined to change that. Yet, it would just annoy him more for her to be mad about something that petty.

George thought Emily looked great for thirty-four, though he wished she would dress less like a teenager. In her painted on jeans and stilettos, she looked on the prowl. He was beginning to feel like the babysitter again. Maybe he should make her a tray of milk and cookies. Her antics didn't just turn him into a wet blanket, they aged him emotionally. George stroked the red tassels on the bookmark lodged in the middle of his hardback.

He raked his brain to remember... was their initial reaction to one another purely physical from the start or did he ever really love this woman? Which came first? Or is it possible to force, to *believe* one or the other kind of attraction to appear? To will it into being? To paste smooth hearts of contentment over uneven, abrasive memories they had created in each other?

Though George readily admitted that Emily was not the only reason for their lackluster marriage, he really did not want the torment, the hassle, or the defeat of a divorce. This could be fixed. It could.

Emily dragged in the next room, turning the television volume up almost all the way even though it was at a tacky advertisement. She locked eyes with George just once as she did this, flipping her hair and lowering the levels to normal just as her favorite soap actor made his entrance.

The doorbell chimed happily, slicing awkwardly into the stilted mood of the house. Emily lifted her iron grasp from Darby and he quickly ran away while he could. When the icing pink packages were loaded inside, Emily stared down the exhausted delivery boy.

"What are you waiting for? A tip? Ha. You were late."

How embarrassing, George thought, overhearing. *Did she order pizza or something?*

George walked through the entry hall on his way to the kitchen for a drink, and stopped short of the mauve mountain of packages. He was speechless.

Somehow the poor delivery boy seemed to know that there was no need to try to argue for a pittance with someone wearing that particular shade of red lipstick.

"They were gifts, honey, see?" His wife held up some curly ribbon. "From Cindy." George groaned. He started to remind her that she had tried this trick two weeks ago, but why should he bother? If she wanted to lie, fine. Emily racked up phone bills to her sister Cindy in London, but, as Emily told him, Cindy was always too busy with work to take the time to come and visit in person.

He had met her briefly at events surrounding the wedding, but that was all. She didn't seem like a very talkative sort, though Emily and she could certainly jabber on. He guessed it was a just a sister thing. George was glad that Emily had a confident, at least. Even if it wasn't him at the moment. Maybe someday it would be. He resolved to try harder.

***

There was a cautious knock on Simon's door. Typing away with earphones in place, he was oblivious to the world except that of the two main characters in the novel he was reviewing for *The Times*, typing as fast as he could. The knock evolved from cautious to anxious. The rhythm playing in Simon's ears sounded off, he changed tracks, and then became conscious that the offbeat was a knock.

He wished that Yolanda had not finished so early this afternoon. Simon hated to answer the door. It seemed to perpetually catch him off guard. He slipped off his worn robe. When new, it was a dark royal blue but now was closer to the indigo hue of lightly stonewashed denim.

Tiptoeing and avoiding the especially noisy boards in the floor, he drew nearer to the door like a ghost. Could whoever it was see him in the peephole? George interrupted his thoughts. "It's me, Simon, open up, for heaven's sake."

Simon turned the bolt, and created a small gust of wind with the speed at which he opened the weighty door.

"Hey, George. Let me get you a drink. What'll you have? I have all the same stuff stocked that I always do, um... let me check the fridge. C'mon in."

George passed over the threshold with less vigor than Simon was used to. He knew it must be something with Emily again. Those were the only times that the expression on George's face was a sort of rigid sadness, an unchanging stillness loitering in his eyes. Barely even blinking.

"Anything's fine, thanks." Simon brought him what George usually ordered for himself, a sparkling water with a lime slice. Although Simon didn't care much for sodas, or anything carbonated for that matter, he had lately gotten into the habit of keeping a few chilled for George's increasingly frequent visits.

"Who's the new doorman?" George asked. Simon was surprised that George had noticed such a detail in the trance he was in.

"Oh, I think he's just a sub. He's been here a week. Some vacation Reilly must be having. Edmund's his name."

"He sure did ignore me into the ground. Then I felt stared at. He opened the door, all right, but he was looking straight into space. Never met my eyes. Reilly always remembered my name. I liked him. This new guy sort of reminded me of someone. Can't put my finger on it though... Really did make me feel... kind of watched, in a weird way...."

When Simon thought George was finished ranting, or should be at any rate, he struggled to conjure up a way to console him. What has she done this time? Now she's got him hallucinating about the doorman.

"Of all the innocent bystanders, George. Think about what you're saying. Wild guess, but is it about Emily?"

"How ever did you come to that far fetched conclusion, Sherlock?" George laughed weakly, lingered in the silence he'd just caused, and finally offered, "We're going to work it out."

Jessica D. Lovett

Simon carelessly started to shake his head to indicate the imminent negative, and then realized the consequence of such an action. He stopped himself before the snipped gesture soaked into the conversation, afraid George would get the wrong idea. Simon didn't want his friend to lose all hope, even if it was misplaced. He could transplant it later, as long as it stayed intact.

***

Maddy Bryson stared at her blinking cursor, tuning out the churning office. "What are you waiting for?" her cheeky colleague sneered, pulling up to her desk. Kirby Holmes began to inspect her neat stacks of papers in mock seriousness as she turned her gaze to him. "Alright, alright. I'll leave you alone, Bryson. Just don't give me one of your 'professional relationship' speeches. I'm not in the mood."

As he finally trailed off, he offered up one more plight, "How about some coffee? Isn't your shift over in a few?" Maddy did not move a muscle, secretly wishing that he would keel over. "I'll take that as a 'no' then. Maybe tomorrow," he stopped and smiled.

No sign from Maddy. Not a slight change in expression. Then, Kirby practically skipped back to her desk and plopped down on one knee. "Pleeeaase?" The way Kirby tended to whiningly drag out each syllable as long as possible when asking Maddy for something – which he did often enough – annoyed her.

"Kirby… though I do appreciate the fact that you are inclined to be romantically interested in me, and see me as a potential 'girlfriend,'" Maddy used this term with particular disgust, "I have no choice but to beg, yes, beg to differ. Frankly, there is no reason to introduce a relationship such as this into my life at this time. There is no need. No need whatsoever. Your offer does flatter me, really it does."

Kirby had dramatically wilted, but Maddy knew he wasn't too injured. She had given him harsher tongue-lashings than that. He let out an exaggerated sigh. "Someday, Bryson. Someday you'll change your mind, and I intend to be standing on this very square of tile when you do."

There was a long pause. Maddy was not amused. She had provided more than a hint, and as usual this guy was obtuse. "Alrighty, I'll bribe you then," Kirby grinned, "If you go out with me for one week I'll keep you informed on this big story I'm typing up for Maxwell."

Maddy rolled her eyes and threw her head back, sending a loose wisp of chocolate hair flying. Kirby flinched, "Well…" "I don't need Blaine Maxwell's leftovers, thank you very much." At this, Kirby gave up at least for the moment. Yet, he had made her curious. Blaine always got assigned juicier stories then she did. *What could he be up to*, she wondered.

***

Buzz. Pause. Buzz, buzzzzz. "State your business." Simon aimed his voice into the little call box posted by the front door. He hated it when the doorman got off duty.

"Don't you know my signature ring yet?" George sounded like a flat soda.

"I though we agreed on buzzity-buzz-buzz."

"Simon, let me in, really." The lock clicked open and George trudged into the empty hallway. He found himself being invaded by familiar thoughts – how homely and drab the beige interior was, how much he wished the powers that be would replace the so-called modern art... As George waited for the elevator, one particular piece of art caught his attention. "What is that supposed to be?" he wondered aloud.

George felt part of his sadness remain on ground level as he slid higher into the air, watching the elevator lights climb through the chain of lit up numbers out of the corner of his eye. After what seemed like a small eternity, the elevator stopped on the fifth floor. Several doors down from the elevator, Simon had left the door of his apartment unlocked.

"What'll ya have, George? I've got the usual stash," Simon called out from the kitchen.

"Oh, water, I guess, thank...." George threw his tired shell into the overstuffed leather couch, letting the impact cut off the "s" in "thanks."

"What? That's it? Water and what else? Hey, I've got some Sprite and lime for you, you know I can't stand the stand the stuff, all that corn syrup," Simon coaxed lightly.

"No, not today. I'm afraid I'm not good company today. It's..."

"Emily," Simon thought.

"Emily," George completed.

"She's... well..." George stalled.

"In one of her famous moods," Simon vocalized.

"Yeah, Simon, how'd you guess?" George almost let loose a small, stifled laugh but caught it in midair.

"Me casa is sue casa," Simon attempted. "Hey, it's only three o'clock. Have you called in yet?"

"Oh! Agnes! Thanks. Just a second." George frantically mined his pockets for his cell phone.

Simon brought in their drinks, presenting George with a fresh bottle of Sprite and not the water he'd asked for, thinking that that's what he really and truly wanted, something fizzy, and then cleared away a notepad and a couple of paperbacks before hunkering down into his easy chair, scanning the textured wall to appear occupied as he watched George's stream of consciousness flood into a surging wall between them.

"Agnes? Yes. Yes. No, I...yes. That's right." George nodded into the phone.

Simon tried to soak up George's mood as he silently observed the outwardly one-sided conversation. He could hear a muffled version of Agnes' prim voice cascading through the phone.

"Tomorrow? Of course I will. Yes. No, I'll...yeah. You know the number."

chapter 4

MADDY GENTLY DRIFTED along the line between being only just asleep and blearily awake watching Humphrey Bogart, secretly longing for long twill trench coats and felt fedoras that were barely slanted to one side to have a fashion comeback. A man never offered a lady his monogrammed silk handkerchief when she was crying anymore. Or even a wrinkled tissue. Come to think of it, women never really cried in public to give men the opportunity. Maddy guessed it wasn't worth uprooting her terribly rational reputation to test her theory.

Contemplating this, she descended deeper into unconsciousness. A dream arose into her mind like rising smoke rings, dissolving all traces of wakefulness just as smoke becomes one with the air around it. In her dream, Maddy was being stalked by a tall, shadowy figure. Running and running with all her might, she fell into an opaque puddle in an endless alley. Her skin was scratched from the tiny sharp edges of the gravel that made up the pavement. Maddy tried to remember to breathe as her heart rate steadily picked up momentum, punctuated by earsplitting gunshots echoing out into the blackness.

Suddenly on the run again, she ducked into an ornate but neglected building and started racing up the creaky wooden stairs. In mid-sprint, she kicked off her satin pumps. Her logic caught up with her delirium...why am I trapping myself upstairs? At the edge of the hall was a door with a frosted glass window painted in stencil to say, "Grant, Gable, & Bogart. Private Investigators." A sigh of relief had scarcely begun to escape her lips when she felt, not heard, a bullet enter her left shoulder. Cringing, she tried to capture the blood as it abandoned its intended course through her veins.

Maddy woke up with a start, and without hesitation inspected her hands in the dim light. She felt the sensations of the dream overflowing into reality. Was she bleeding? She felt it! It's real blood! Shrieking, Maddy jabbed her hand under the lampshade in a harried attempt locate the switch.

When the light flooded the room, she glanced down to see broken glass swallowed by a puddle of water on the floor beside the nightstand. The left side of the bed was wet, including her arm and the sleeve of her nightgown. Evidently, knocking the cup of water over in the night had caused her imagination to take over. The comforter, extra blanket, and sheets had all been kicked off and sent into a sprawling spiral half on the floor and half clinging to one side of her bed.

***

"So you're saying she hates children, too?" Simon sighed into their strewn-out conversation, feeling the emotional strain that he always experienced whenever Emily's soap opera-esque antics were elaborated upon. He never understood what George had seen in her in the first place... How could he stay married to such a preening prima donna?

Simon was rendered speechless whenever George asked for advice like this. He could not seem to wrap his mind around the situation. It all seemed cut and dry to him, especially since George had started to suspect that Emily was being unfaithful to him. Two words perpetually tried to jab their way out of his mouth: leave her. *She's bad for you. She makes you feel miserable. Simply leave her.*

Couldn't George have had some other addiction that was easier to deal with, something physical and real, like caffeine, alcohol, or pills? Besides, the way Emily pushed George around hurt Simon, too. After all, they had been close friends for years and years. Yet, nothing changed. These characteristic rifts always ended in the same, unresolved way. George would apologize and admit everything was his fault even if he hadn't tilted his ever-present halo of righteousness even slightly.

George was a golden statue of kindness, and it boggled Simon's mind. Simon resented Emily more and more each day, more than George ever showed in their most serious conversations. George would only confide his rational feelings and thoughts, how hurt he was, and how much he struggled to understand what was going on in that mind of hers. He never gossiped, never whined, and never complained about Emily in a blatant way.

Back in college, George and Emily's engagement had been a blow to Simon. After all, he had only met Emily a couple of times, and George didn't care to ask his opinion of her! Next thing Simon knew, George was in his dorm talking to him about being the best man at the wedding that was to take place in a fleeting three months. That seemed odd as well.

Simon had initially perceived Emily as the kind of girl who would be wedding-obsessed since childhood, with bridal gowns and tuxes for her dolls. Such a rushed wedding date seemed to clash with her disposition. Well, maybe not.

She probably had it all mapped out on paper from age twelve, and now there was nothing planning-wise left to be done except mailing out the invitations and receiving gifts. To top it off, George would heed none of his sincere warnings. George just saw Simon's arguments as the standard best-friend-slash-dedicated-bachelor commentary.

George gave Simon a verbal shake back into their current situation. "It's not that Emily hates kids entirely. Well, actually she just might. She hasn't said so in so many words." George slumped further back into the chair, bending his frame into the same curvature of the lines on his furrowed brow.

This confession stole a little something from George's soul, but he still had to let the words escape him. At any rate, he had the feeling that Simon wasn't all that surprised to hear it.

Simon hesitated, "What makes you think that, George? I mean, maybe you're reading stuff into her words. If you don't mind me saying so, I don't think she is capable of successfully hinting at anything."

"Yes, subtlety is not her strong suit."

"Not by a long shot. She's a...Doberman," Simon whispered these last words.

"I know it. She is. You're right, absolutely right."

"And you are her self-appointed chew toy," Simon wanted to append but did not. He counted to ten, and then continued on, attempting to be encouraging but deteriorating instead, "Since you know it, have you thought that maybe it's better not to have kids? I mean, they might..." Simon paused then, sensing George taking in a deep breath as if getting ready to speak.

"Be just like Emily," George interrupted slowly, his eyes widening.

"I hate to sound like a jerk, I really do."

"I came here to hear honesty. I don't get that at home. Or at work, really."

Simon waited.

"And, for that matter, I don't remember what honesty is. It seems like that I give in about everything, for the sake of being a nice guy, and I never get what I want. Is it being honest to be nice?"

"I don't know..."

"I can't even complain anymore, except to you." George rubbed his forehead.

"What do you..."

"Agnes doesn't even know how I like my coffee, Simon. She's my secretary!"

"Is that really important?"

"Maybe it is! Is it all my own fault anyway? That I've stopped trying to rationally explain anything to my irrational wife? Is that lying?"

"It's not your fault that Emily is like this, George."

Simon had reached the boiling point. Maybe it was partly George's fault – his fault for marrying her in the first place. He was worried about George, certainly, but there's only so much room in his psyche for emotional intimacy at any given time. Especially for such a touchy subject. Simon racked his brain for a subject change. George had said the word "work." That was just the ticket.

"Since you mentioned it, how is life in that real world of yours?"

"Chemi-Life? Do you want a candid answer or that of the faithful employee?"

"Is that rhetorical, George?"

"Sinking. Or sunk. Depends on how you look at it."

"What?" Simon didn't expect the conversation to take such a nosedive, either.

"It goes without saying, well that's obsolete – here I am saying it – but, this is all privileged information. If the stockholders found out, more importantly, if Clayton found out I said anything," George finished his sentence without finishing his thoughts.

"Now, when have I ever…"

"Never, Simon, of course not. I'm just ranting."

***

Edmund Hopkins wondered how long he was going to have to pose as Edmund the helpful, monotonous doorman of this apartment building before he was able figure out what to do next. This job was the closest he could get. It was a long shot, but though he had not been able to uncover Emily's unlisted address or phone numbers, he had been successful in discretely following her husband after work. He didn't want to follow him all the way down the winding, solitary road to their home and look like a stalker. What would he do once he got there, anyway? At least this way, he can begin to be "friends" with George and gradually figure out a way to talk to Emily again without her immediately shutting him out.

Edmund had begun to feel sorry for her yuppie husband, Dr. George Morris. Edmund had seen George several times a week with increasing length to his visits, scurrying to his college friend, writer Simon Kincade, for comfort.

Emily must be just like her old self, judging from poor Morris's parade of bedraggled expressions. No career could produce despondence such as that. After so much had happened to their family after she graduated from college, his precocious little girl had become a terribly unpleasant, brassy, and whiney adult.

Still, posing as a doorman was a far cry from the previous posts his career had taken him to. At any rate, even if he was unsuccessful and had to go back to Texas, at least he was having an interesting enough time in this new job.

***

"So, you swear to me, Simon, you won't say a thing."

"If you don't trust me, then fine. I'll..."

George interrupted Simon's huff. Taking a hefty breath, he began, without further hesitation.

"Like I've mentioned before, Chemi-Life's main revenue comes from getting the right drugs to the right audience. Some we make alone, but some of the manufacturing responsibilities of the medicines are shared with a smaller company out of Jersey... Smithson Pharmaceutical."

"Uh, huh," Simon nodded.

"Well, something groundbreaking happened when they were working together. They opened up the Pandora's box of moral pharmacology with something entirely new: a 'smart' drug that not only improves cognitive processes but makes people nice! It's like a religion pill. Makes people want to do the 'right thing' in all situations."

"Whose definition of 'right thing' is that?"

"Good point. Yeah. That would make a difference. Well, to make a long story shorter, Smithson got greedy. Greedy and impatient. They stopped testing adequately to get the meds on the pharmacy shelves quicker. They thought they knew their stuff well enough for that, and the premature ad campaigns didn't help matters either."

Simon waited, soaking all of it in. He got up and walked around, all of a sudden lacking something to do to use up energy. George's eyes followed him around the room, not stopping the floodgates of his story after going to the tremendous emotional effort of starting it.

"People were asking their doctors for these new products after seeing them on television, thinking it was just an elevated cup of coffee with a little anti-depressant thrown in, before they'd been actually tested for a long enough period of time to see what other side effects might incur. All these silly ads with families and people jogging with their golden retrievers! Sunlit sidewalks!"

He stopped for a moment and took another noticeably deep breath, looking like he desperately needed a pastoral, sunlit sidewalk jog with a loyal pooch more than anyone else in the world. Simon had nothing to add, so George kept on.

"Smithson responded to the rush unethically. Before my reassignment, I had to talk to those people. Believe me, they have no scruples. The media doesn't know it yet, but there have been quite a few deaths. It's only a matter of time before...."

The color drained from George's face as he attempted to hide the prophetic grief that accompanied this last unfinished sentence. To escape, he aimed his eyes toward the open window. The gray, cement view didn't give him much to escape to.

"Deaths?!" Simon interjected, his mouth involuntarily gaping wide. "Wait a minute! Doesn't the FDA test these things?"

"Ha. They generally trust the test results that they receive from scientists assigned to it."

"Well?"

"Sometimes the results differ from test to test and the less favorable results are... um... kept under wraps. The silver lining results are the ones that the people see. Sometimes drugs are tested and tested until a positive result is squeezed out of it, something to write articles about and give press to."

"That's horrifying."

"Yes, it is."

"I think I'll stick to chamomile tea, Dr. George, no offense!"

"None taken. I thank God every day that I was 'promoted' away from all that. I think they didn't want me to get too close, get in the middle of it all and sic my nagging conscience on them, you know? Most of this month I've been stuck dealing with a kids' cereal account, spending my lifeblood to lower the sugar content and up the vitamins to appease the other execs and the parents." A weak laugh seeped through his closed lips.

"Some way to use your degree, Dr. Morris. Picking out prizes for cereal boxes."

"Touché. They need me there at least."

"I thought that so-called 'higher-ups' didn't get shifted around like that."

"Food has chemical engineering involved, too, you know. Nobody ever realizes that. Plus, there are some really cool prizes in those nowadays...."

"Still, George! That's crazy! You've got to say something to... to... someone!"

"I know," George closed his eyes, "I just don't know how right now. Of course Chemi-Life would fire me instantly. And, who would hire me when they found out about all this? People who get hired are those with a clean slate. The rest fall into the oblivion."

"Chemicals, chemicals, chemicals." Simon rubbed his temples, felt a headache coming on, but wasn't about to go grab a generic acetaminophen, given the toxic conversation piling up around him.

"I was two doors down from the lab that birthed the evil stuff, Simon. It'd be easy for Chemi-Life to pin plenty on me if I tried to alert the authorities. I'm sure my name is tied to some of the ingredients they poured into that pill."

Simon was silent. He had stopped rubbing his head but had not moved his hands away, shielding his eyes away from the lights, which seemed suddenly harsh.

"Besides all that, the company is going under. Our stock is being eaten alive. So, yes, back to our original topic, my salary is suffering with the best of them."

"What is Emily's comment about that? They way she shops, you'd think there was an impending clothing famine," Simon attempted to get a laugh. And failed.

"She doesn't know, and won't if I can help it. I'm sure Emily has no idea what I do at Chemi-Life or the magnitude of any of it. The title of Senior Executive tacked on my office door and the accompanying check is the only part of my work that matters to her. She stopped asking how my day went years ago. I stopped asking about her day because I was tired of lies. The biggest bills I forward to my office. Knowing her as I do, there's no telling what Agnes thinks about all that extra mail from home."

chapter 5

MADDY CHUGGED AND sputtered her way into the only available parking slot, taking extra precaution as she eased in. She had circled the lot twice hoping to avoid the torture of parking parallel in such a tight spot, almost ready to sacrifice her comfort and walk the three extra blocks from the empty lot next door in pumps but not quite.

Sighing in sync with the engine as she flipped off the air conditioner to conserve energy at start up, Maddy wished she could afford a new paint job, for dignity at least. The flaking blue paint exposed spots of rust and mini dents made by the haphazard previous owner.

One thought consoled her, though. Soon she'd be able to afford a smart little car, something sophisticated and not too sporty, like a sleek sedan. She planned to find one whose original owners had seen the inside of a carwash once in a while. People had warned her that black cars were too hard to keep clean, and that red cars got stolen and were magnets to cops since they looked fast. Nevertheless, those were the colors she had always been attracted to. Maybe silver would be nice. That would be a happy medium at least, a little racy and a little conservative.

The hand painted sign adorned with rainbow colored, abstract daisies and butterflies welcomed her. "Monarch Lodge"

Jessica D. Lovett

was scrawled in large, ribboning letters. One would never guess
that this was indeed a nursing home and retirement community.
Unlike the rest of the staffers, Maddy had grown out of the desire
to cover life-threatening, fast-paced events.

After college, she had pounced on every heist, suicide attempt, homicide, and bank robbery she could get her hands
on. Now she honestly preferred human-interest stories to long
drawn-out conflicts. It satisfied her to shed light on the good
side of human nature once in a while. One heartfelt story of
kindness seemed to balance out the pages and pages of chaos.

Still, Maddy didn't take these jobs too often. Something
kept her from admitting the pleasure she took at slowing the
pace. What about her hard-nosed reputation? Kirby would have
a heyday if she let down that guard even a little bit. Then again,
he'd have nothing to dangle in front of her as dating bait.

Last March was the last time she had been sent to cover
a jumper. Absentmindedly scratching details of the scene onto
her yellow legal pad, a cry had grabbed her attention. Looking around to locate its owner, she had seen a boy about eight
years old clinging to his mother's flowing skirt. The mother was
shielding the boy's eyes with one handing and fighting the commotion for a cab with the other. At that moment, a rush of guilt
flooded over Maddy's cheeks. How calloused. She felt spineless,
selling this jumper's -- this man's fate for what? To get her name
above another smudged block of text, strewn down the page like
faceless binary computer codes, the ones that always popped up
when something was going wrong? To win another handful of
loyal readers among the ones who scan their discontented eyes
hungrily over words that took her hours to shape?

There was no reason for this. It bothered her for the next
few weeks, images of the child's contorted face, red with tears and

46

genuine sorrow for the impending death of a stranger, haunting her. It played back in her memory in flashes like antique news reels in black and white, the speed churning in and out, unsteady and unreliable. When payday rolled around, Maddy endorsed the check with the cheap pen she always kept in her checkbook, locked the check into the bank shuttle, and sent it away as if it were blood money.

Why did she become a journalist in the first place? Her mother had thought it was important to have a back up plan to the marriage ideal that was in the back of most of her friend's minds, and have the ability to become independent. College could give her that independence slowly, and in a more protected way.

For an eighteen year old who was too impatient to teach, too right-brained for anything remotely connected to mathematics, journalism seemed like an exciting prospect. So, Maddy resolved to be Brenda Starr in taupe, never tan, stockings while she waited to be whisked off her by Mr. Prince Charming, which was naturally going to happen at just any time.

But, who was she kidding? She was good, not great at her job. Maddy had come to be respected in her field, earning it with fresh ideas and a never-say-die attitude. Her coworkers at *The Times* had finally stopped patronizing her, which she had hated. On her nerve-wracked first day there, some stud kid had brazenly hinted to her that the coffee pot was empty. "Fine," she had snapped with a voice not her own, "I drink tea."

Only a little lie. Coffee was a necessity; tea was pure indulgence. The pithy outburst had shaken her up, though. Maddy didn't know her own verbal strength. After finally giving up trying to speak up in grade school, she had become the kid in the back row who never raised her hand yet knew all the answers and had been that way ever since. Whenever that guy had been in the break room when she was, Maddy had reached for Earl Gray and honey, attempting to kill her coffee cravings out of pride.

Thank goodness that nuisance had left for greener pastures within a few months, and given her free reign of the coffeemaker. Men like that intimidated her, and because of that fact, combined with her striking looks and impeccable style, she usually came across as a conceited diva or prima donna instead of the insecure and painfully shy wallflower she really was, struggling to keep afloat while going through the motions.

All of these cast iron defenses were weighing her down more every day. Dipping into her soft suede handbag, Maddy fished out the checkbook pen she'd used at the bank, and flicked it into one of the empty wastebaskets.

***

"Tired Of Lies..." Simon pondered to himself, thinking about the last part of his and George's conversation the day before. Not a bad title for his mystery novel! No, actually, who'd want to read something about being tired and surrounded by lies, that sounds boring and entirely too realistic. People want an escape, don't they?

He still couldn't believe that Chemi-Life would be covering up deaths! He had thought that he had heard Clayton say "death" that time, when he was waiting for George a few days ago.

Wait. Simon realized that he was selfishly ignoring his friend, and with the speed of that realization, he felt a swift wave of guilt slap over him. George went on uninterrupted, sincerely needing to at least air his thoughts to someone. *The man has too many problems*, Simon sighed to himself. Ironically, lamenting over how to "fix" his marriage seemed more important to George than repairing all the Chemi-Life problems. George saw one problem as irreparable and the other sparked with a little bit of hope when both seemed terminally broken to Simon.

At the end of his tirade, George retreated onto his couch, not looking over to Simon or waiting to be followed. Simon didn't know what to do. He didn't feel comfortable in George's interior decorated place. He'd much rather be at home if he had to play psychologist. He knew he should say something.

He searched his thoughts for any tidbits he could pitch into the dithering conversation. This never used to happen. George was the observant, encouraging one; he expected Simon to be happy-go-lucky. Coaxing fun out of dull situations. Suggesting random, spontaneous exploits. When did that stop being his role?

The house reeked of Emily's extravagant tastes, overflowing flower arrangements pulling Simon's eyes from George's plights, not from beauty exactly but out of sheer distraction from their size.

Occasionally, Simon would have to work to uphold George's expectations that Simon was easygoing to the core. It could be hard work! More and more expectations were being hurled at him. Why, in college, they... His thoughts trailed off.

In college... *I'm thinking about that way too much,* he tried to mentally slap himself back into the present. It's just that it was easy to think about, to fall back into. Things were easier then. If only he could've realized it at the time and relished it a bit more instead of being as frazzled as he was, just under the surface.

Oh, well.

Jessica D. Lovett

Simon looked at his watch — nervous habit — before he could catch himself. He hoped George hadn't noticed. He had. He was standing up to leave the room, dejectedly taking the hint that George took it to be.

Simon tried, "Hey, I just realized that it's about dinner time... So, ah... Hungry? Wanna go grab something?" That worked. George had believed his quick save. Good. Simon wasn't hungry in the least, but eating a meal together at least would be less awkward.

They would inevitably have to have excusable moments of silence set aside for chewing, drinking, using a napkin.

"What does that watch inscription say again?" George asked, victoriously fueling the conversation. Simon knew he was doing this, asking him about art, something Simon was passionate about, and willingly took the bait. They had both been searching for something.

" 'A great artist is always before his time or behind it.' George Moore."

"So where are you, Simon?"

"Where am I how?"

"You know, are you before your time or behind it?"

"I'm not a 'great artist.' I don't know if I'm even a mediocre artist, or one at all for that matter."

"What is an artist anyway, except one who produces art? And that's what you do. You write. And, writing is art, right?"

"That doesn't mean anything. An artist is essentially a channel who..."

"Fine. Whatever you say. I'm not in the mood for this."

George murmured something that sounded like it could have been appended to his last sentence, but Simon couldn't really hear him.

Secretly this saddened Simon. He was quite enjoying this, being set up for a bit of encouragement which he desperately needed, though he was beginning to see that any encouragement that either of them could uncover from their inner depths needed to be shoveled into George's burning, famished wood stove of a spirit.

"Do you, as a self-proclaimed non-artistic person, see writing as a 'real' job?"

"I told you. I'm not in the mood, Simon." Silence. More silence.

Simon's dreams of becoming a writer, capital "W," had slowly started quietly dying away at the hands of shattering teachers, rude acquaintances, well-meaning friends... the list goes on, but most of all, his own self-doubt was at the root of any writer's block he'd ever experienced, and that was a great deal stronger than anything anyone could say to, or at, him. It took much more to beat it down.

He pushed himself so low into the ground that he needed straight up praise from others, not to be narcissistic, but to raise him back up to a normal working level.

Sometimes, on days when he could push back the enemy far enough to give himself adequate space to think and stop fighting, the words would just come. He would feel traces of his biggest dream, to be one of those people who were given words, a conduit to something higher than himself. A muse. God maybe.

He wasn't sure, but he knew that in the few and far between flashes of light that he received, like seemingly random lightning strikes in a clear and cloudless day, that in those moments he wrote first and found the meaning later.

To him, that, in essence, was what turned someone writing, someone searching for words to fill a page, into a Writer (no doubts, capital "W"). Into someone who runs out of pages. A real writer is someone bigger than himself who writes more than he knows. A writer touches more emotions than even his own psyche consists of, Simon pondered. He wished that someone close to him could understand, could empathize, and not just think, however secretly, that Simon was just lazy.

He was not lazy. He was *trying* to be an artist. To win the right to look in the mirror and see himself as a writer. To feel that singularly significant feeling of someone with swathes of pages surrounding him, pages that he can be proud of.

Simon held the limp pieces of this dream in his hands every day as he carried around legal pads or a laptop everywhere he went, searching for warmth, pressing in his perked ear in harder and harder to find a hidden heartbeat and reassure himself that his dream hadn't died away completely. He'd endeavor to sustain himself, saying there would always be somebody better at writing than him and always somebody worse. It never worked, however, because he wanted to be the best, however silly and childish that that dream might seem.

Being average, assuring himself that he could reach for average, did not help one bit. It actually disheartened him. Why did people always say that to him? Why would he dignify it by recounting it so often? He'd be sitting there, upset, and make the mistake of saying something about not finding the words to write or worrying about writing, and that's what so many people had used as their retort. Someone would always be better, someone always worse.

Why not just say something like, "You can do it!" or "I have faith in you," or if they had just read pages of his, say something the equivalent of "You write well." Something as simple as that would be a super-luxe spa treatment for his weary soul. He felt like an obedient puppy that always came when called, always sat, always rolled over and never got that elusive milk-bone.

George broke into Simon's mental tirade, "You've told me a million times about how Shakespeare was severely under appreciated in his time and all that."

"Not Shakespeare. He *was* appreciated. Famous."

"Whomever it was that you told me."

"Yeah, well, there are plenty of them." That's all Simon could muster. He was still lost in sinewy thoughts as they slowly tapered off and loosened their tight grip.

"Well… Shakespeare isn't appreciated in our time, though. Like how that some people even believe that the poor guy was too puny to have even written his own works! The most brilliant author, and no cheers."

"Yeah…" Simon repeated, trying not to sound as crestfallen as he really was.

"Consider yourself speeched at."

"'Speeched' isn't a word."

"Fine. You know what I mean," George raised his eyebrows.

"Awww, come on!" By this, George thought that Simon meant, "Come on and use the right word," when what he really meant was "Come on and give me a little more encouragement than that. You were doing fine."

It didn't occur to either of them to clarify themselves. They just took it personally, even though wrong, and took it in stride.

When he could tell that he was not to be nourished with any more words from George, after donating plenty of silence to their talk for George to jump into, Simon withdrew into thoughts of his novel. He pictured the glossy dust jacket, saw his name on the cover in bold print, felt the pleasing weight of the pages press into his fingers.

He kept these thoughts in the forefront, plenty enough for his mind to feast upon, after he had left George, all the way back to his apartment building, floating through the Edmund's compulsory greeting, who he had actually began to take a liking to, and up the moody elevator, past the ritual of unlocking his door – carefully as to not scratch the new bolt – and all the way through the boot up process of his laptop.

Though he usually pushed the on button and then left to do other things as to not waste moments while the computer was logging on, this time, he just sat there. The minutes flew by, as his mind was suspended elsewhere. Simon was surprised to look up and see his desktop completely loaded up when he usually eyed it impatiently for what seemed like forever.

Simon carefully eyed the last words he had typed into the story, hoping for inspiration. His main character had yet to be named. He kept typing "MAIN CHARACTER" and "GIRL" and on and on, simply because he could not think of good enough character names. The ones he thought of always seemed too contrived to use. He thumbed through the phone book, hoping to get more realistic sounding name ideas, to no avail.

He heard a key scratching at the door and Yolanda's scuttled footsteps going into the kitchen.

"C'mon Simon, don't you have any coffee that doesn't smell like roasted dirt?" Yolanda called out to Simon in his bedroom, sticking her head out from the kitchen. Simon let out half of a chuckle as he sauntered into the kitchen in sock feet. She took one more whiff of the afternoon cappuccinos she was habitually making for the two of them and shuddered dramatically.

"Ewww…," skewed her face into a pursed knot.

"It's supposed to be very good... full-bodied, complex," he offered.

"According to who?" she countered, hands on her hips.

"According to The Coffee Cup salesperson."

"Well, they don'know what they're talking about."

Simon loved the easy dynamic of their shared bantering. No baggage or tensions... No guilt-trips. Only lightheartedness.

Yolanda laughed, still in anti-smoky coffee mode. Simon added, "As long as it inspires wakefulness, I'm fine," and at that, she jokingly agreed to "give it a shot." It took Simon a minute to get her meaning. "Give the coffee a 'shot,' get it?" Yolanda had said again, proudly laughing at her own pun on espresso.

Martin Ortega – must be a happy, happy man to be married to such a light-hearted lady, he supposed. Simon wondered how he ever lived without Yolanda Ortega and im-mediately knew the answer... he had lived much messier and much lonelier.

***

George had gone to sleep alone, aware of Emily's footsteps downstairs and the television's muted noises. Sometime in the night he had been somewhat aware of Emily's creeping under the covers in slow motion, in a kind attempt not to wake him. George had felt as she eased her tense muscles, one by one, into the mattress until her entire weight gave way into the softness. He had eased down with her, easily at first, and then he had stopped himself, halfway worried that she'd notice that he was awake and want to talk. She hadn't noticed.

He could hear her snoring a little bit, so George knew that she was deeply asleep. Several hours had passed with George wavering in and out of wakefulness, glad to feel her feminine presence without feeling her words jutting out against him. Just as he was edging a little closer to her, considering how close he could get to her warmth without bothering her, she shrieked, leaping upright with a jolt.

The lightning bolt shriek had shot into the darkness, armed with desperate sounds that sounded like the words "not him," but George wasn't too sure. He took it to mean that she did not want him touching her, even in an asleep state. He saw her beautiful face telling the silent witnesses in her dream, "Not George!"

"I'm sorry, Emily! I didn't mean to..."

"No, George, no. It's not you. It's me. I was having a nightmare."

He sighed, more relieved than he could voice. They had been here before. He could deal with any number of nightmares, as long as they were not about him.

"The gunshot one?"

"Yes."

"Do you remember anything else about it? Just one gunshot?"

"No."

George could tell she was lying by her quick answer and vacant stare. A random gunshot going off in the distance did not sound like a scary nightmare to him.

"It might help if you talked about it with me, Emily."

"No. I'm okay. Really. Go back to sleep. I'm fine."

George tried to go back to sleep but he could feel the slight vibrations in the mattress betraying the fact that Emily was crying. She always tightened her stomach muscles when she was attempting to hide her crying, as if her they could reach up to her eyes and turn off their flow. George wished that she could just tell him. There's no way it was so bad that she couldn't at least tell him what she had been dreaming about. You can't very well blame someone for their nightmares, holding them accountable somehow for the dark thoughts that took them unawares. When had he betrayed her so terribly to make her feel that she could not trust him more than that?

***

Maddy followed the florescent light patches with her eyes as they trailed down the white marble floors like illuminated puddles, fighting the urge to jump into them. Every third tile in front of her was brimming with the reflections of the lights above it. Yes, hospitals had white floors and were well lit like Monarch Lodge was, but hospitalization seemed like a foreign concept to this buoyant place. Maddy rubbed her eyes, still a little bit sleepy. She didn't usually do early morning interviews if she could help it.

There were ornate arrangements of bird of paradise flowers and others Maddy did not recognize. She had to touch the leaves to see if the vivid, dustless plants were real or only plastic, or maybe silk. Oddly, the fact that they were fake did not take anything away from their stateliness. In the distance Maddy heard what she had come here for.

A jazzy trumpet sang and trilled into the freshly painted halls. The sound morphed into a smooth, free serenade. Maddy half expected the nurses to break into a choreographed chorus number in their identical white outfits and their all white but all different styles of tennis shoes as the playing purified the air and bounced off each hard surface, resonating and making

Jessica D. Lovett

everything holy in its own way. After a soft refrain and trailing off of the last notes, applause ended the melody.

"Play it again, Jed!"

"Encore!"

As Maddy wandered down the corridors, she inspected the diverse art unified by substantial oak frames, mostly nameless Impressionists. Standing inside one of the wreathed doorways, a wispy lady in a yellow chenille robe had the expression of someone who had just wished on a star.

"Bravo," the lady whispered into her silent room. Maddy raised her eyes and began to say hello, but the lady scampered into her room as if frightened by such an intrusion into her moment of introspection.

At last she reached room three twenty-eight. What Maddy saw overwhelmed her. The wide open doorway exposed a wall plastered with a loosely structured collage of Navy emblems, photos of children of all ages, plaques, awards, and two barely tarnished medals in a shadow box.

At second glance she distinguished that many of the pictures were the same few kids, these photos chronicling their lives as they got older. In an indescribable way age did not change them, their faces and particular set of expressions exactly remained the same.

The golden sunlight filtered upon the array like a spotlight, and Maddy's glance traced the light to its source. Angled toward the window was a brick red recliner, the bell of a silver trumpet rested on its armrest. As the chair spun around, Maddy met the face of a – if it could be possible – clean-shaven Santa Claus.

"Come on in, young lady." Somehow when this voice called her a "young lady" it was disarming, not belittling like it was when her mother's Thursday night bridge game friends had called her that. Maddy felt six years old and she liked it.

This man was garlanded with opulent life experiences and she genuinely wanted to hear his story after meeting his amber eyes, now more than when she had first been presented with this assignment.

"You must be Miss Bryson."

Maddy's shyness fled as she found herself drawn closer to him, wishing she could really be six right now and sit in his lap to beg for a fairy-tale without any qualm or hesitation.

"Mr. Engle, it is such a pleasure to meet you. *The Times* is so lucky to have this opportunity to share your story."

"Please, call me Jed."

"Sure, and I'm Madeline. Maddy."

At this, she held out her hand. Jed Engle's toned grip surprised her. The door opened and a nurse walked in holding a tray with a tiny plastic cup of water, two pills, and a newspaper. After a brief exchange, Jed took his pills quickly and told the nurse to have a nice day as she left, her back to him.

"Let's get started, shall we? Do you mind if I record our conversation?"

"My, no," Jed was impressed by her tiny digital tape recorder, "I sure could've used one of those babies back in the Pacific! Whew!"

chapter 6

SCREAMING, UNWASHED CHILDREN staring him down from their grimy seatbelted perch atop the metal carts. Little old ladies accusing him of blocking their aisle. Soccer moms with leftover vengeance from their kid's lost game, barely missing his toes with their raging carts. These were the images that were instantly conjured when Simon thought of going to Super-Mart. He was of the opinion that it should be declared an official war zone.

Worse, though, was the fact that he *had* to go. He was forced to go. There are some things that cannot be found at smaller local stores, and besides, it was exponentially cheaper. He was beginning to think, as he navigated his clicking, squeaky cart through the freezer section - squeezing around an arguing couple to snag a couple frozen pizzas and then realizing that they were supreme pizzas instead of the plain pepperoni that he had been aiming for - that paying extra to go to a smaller place was looking more and more worth it with each passing moment.

Idea! Maybe he could pay Yolanda to go shopping for him! Aw, she wouldn't do it, he mused, sadly. Not for a huge raise. She had her dignity... her pride! How did she ever do her shopping at such a place for the four in her family? Shopping for one was enough.

It must take all afternoon just to hunt and gather enough to feed them all for a couple of days in such a medieval gauntlet. And, she would have to go with a checker if she was getting a lot, and not use the self-checkout system, and that would just be crazy to wait in line behind cart after overflowing cart! He'd have to ask her. Maybe she brought a book with her to help weather the storm. Yet, no one could read anything in those lines, surrounded by such a garish racket.

All of a sudden, lost in his own thoughts, thinking that maybe he could use this supermarket angst in his novel, he almost ran over someone with his cart. Upon recovering his steering and turning around again, he saw that it turned out to be a very pretty someone. She was examining the varieties of flavored ground coffee and looked as if she had narrowed it down to Swiss Chocolate or Vanilla Hazelnut, one in each French manicured hand, taking turns being whiffed.

The girl didn't seem to notice that she had almost been run over. He hadn't touched her, after all. Oh, well. He tried to retreat back into his previous, comfortingly mundane thoughts and failed.

A girl like that would never notice him – case in point. She was probably too young to carry on an interesting conversation anyway. But, how much did that really matter? Was conversation really that important? Simon scolded himself for having such thoughts and moved on.

***

"Flighty?!"
"Well, Miss Bryson, there are just no…"

"That's Ms. Bryson to you, Mr. Norton." The gray-tinged face of the editor stared into Maddy's, and his practiced poker face revealed nothing to her searching eyes. One wouldn't be able to guess his age; he looked weathered enough to be well over seventy, but yelled out speeches on the ethics of journalism and journalistic pride with enough vigor to be twenty years younger than that.

He seemed to treat Maddy with unusually soft kid gloves, which angered and confused her to no end. She would have rather been yelled at with the rest of the reporters than treated as a weakling.

"Your stories have just gotten flighty lately... and your writing style capricious." He ended this statement by holding eye contact with her, challenging, waiting for a reply. This startled her and she stopped short. No one had ever called her "flighty" before. Her! Serious, cynical, hard-nosed - yes! But, definitely not "flighty." Yes, she had to admit that she may get overly excited about things sometimes, but that was because of her moral nature! Her belief system!

"So, you're saying I'm unintelligent, Mr. Norton?" After saying this, she realized that she should have taken back the "so" since that, in itself, sounded even more unintelligent.

"No. You know I'm not. I'm not saying that at all. I'm saying that there are things going on in this world, big things, miserable things, that you are oblivious to. Pain and suffering that you can only..."

"All the more reason to bring light into that darkness!" Maddy interrupted, wishing that she hadn't, "And, I'm not oblivious! I...I..."

She wanted to say that she was more aware of the world around her than depressive Norton ever could be in his wildest

Jessica D. Lovett

dreams. Maddy could feel the intensity in things Norton seemed to just ignore. To overcome, to look it in the face and not continually drown oneself in misery was a sign of strength and wisdom, not one of weakness or naivety.

Why couldn't he see that? Good thing the office door was shut. Kirby kept intently peering over, looking as if he was trying to read their lips or something.

And, where was that creepy Blaine guy, she wondered, halfheartedly. He seemed to always be looming. She did a quick sweep of her desk to make sure that none of her story outlines were vanishing from view and that no one was snooping on her desktop. She hadn't had time to shut it down when Norton had summoned her from the back of the room. It was that kind of office.

"Your coworkers have been talking. They say that you only talk with them about basics. Conversations about just the trivial things. That you're not grounded, Bryson."

It annoyed her when people, especially those in her field, talked in prolonged incomplete sentences. Maddy wanted to say that she found nothing interesting enough in her coworkers to invest even a pittance of intimacy in any of them, and that she was only talking to them out of politeness, not out of respect.

"I'm afraid I don't understand, Mr. Norton. My coworkers have not complained to me. I believe that conversation between professionals should not get too personal."

She didn't mean it to sound as it did, to infer that Norton himself was edging toward being too personal with her. Her remark took him aback, making him pause briefly.

Maddy took the silence after leaving it alone for a significant amount of time, giving him every opportunity to add a retort. "My work is turned in before the deadlines, is it not? And, in the quality expected of *The Times?*"

"Yes, but there has been a thread of the emotional in it."

"Isn't passion what drives journalism?"

"Yes, but within limits. Showing yourself to your readers is a sign of an immature writer."

"I'm afraid that I have to disagree with you."

"Yes, yes. I like you, Ms. Bryson. I really do. But, I'm afraid that I'm going to have to..."

"Ah! Fire me?!" she thought, famished for his next word and dreading it all the same.

"...begin a probationary period, to review your work more closely." Norton finished, much to her relief and horror. In a way, deep down, she would have rather just been fired. Started anew. But, that would have jaded her fledgling résumé.

"Fine. Thank you, sir."

The conversation got dull after that. Norton pulling out dull assignments for her to cover in a dull way, not allowing any colorful adjectives at all, evidently.

Maddy stormed out to her car, not even caring if anyone else saw it, then realizing that she probably had just added to the immature image Norton had unjustly painted of her.

***

Blaine threw open his car door, not realizing that Maddy could jolt out of the building so quickly, and pitched in the too-large-for-a-pocket knife that he'd used to discretely flatten her front driver's side tire. The tire's thin, worn rubber made it easy to slip the point of the blade between the tread. The air had

Jessica D. Lovett

gone out quietly, Blaine tilting the edge of the blade in an angle to make for a clean escape.

Maddy ignored him as he strutted next to his car with one hand stroking the shiny hood, completely unaware of the way it made him look like a used car salesman flaunting tired wares.

"Hey, there…" he called out, forcing his voice to fit into nonchalant tones. Maddy turned and gave him a short, unfriendly wave, unaccompanied ambiguously by either a glance or a smile. This was more out of shyness than out of rudeness, but the two reactions, coming from her, resembled each other so closely that no one could ever tell which it was and generally ended up choosing the later as the most likely candidate.

"Hey, there, Maddd…eline Bryyy…son," Blaine said again, this time with more feeling, louder and stronger, as he pulled out each letter of her name in a way that made Maddy feel uneasy. It was as if he was being too thorough, too intimate with each of the letters, acting as if he liked saying her name and he intended to keep saying it.

"Mad…e-line…" he tried again, in a lighter, more singsong voice. Obviously, she couldn't get him to stop calling after her so tenaciously by simply ignoring him. It only fueled his ardor.

Her thoughts swarmed, full of possible excuses, as she tried to sort out the best one… "I have a meeting in a few minutes; can't stay and chat," or, one he'd be more likely to identify with, given his overly groomed, overwhelmingly cologned nature, "I've got a hair appointment! Sorry, got to hurry."

After their initial mandatory exchange of hellos, the most unlikely one of these excuses flew from her assaulted lips involuntarily.

"I'm meeting someone for coffee – got to hurry off! Sorry!"

"Well, you won't be 'hurrying off' with that tire," Blaine said jokingly and with altogether too much confidence. He waited for a short, concise beat and added, "Let me give you a lift."

"What? Tire? What do you mean?"

"Take a look yourself. I saw it when I was walking past."

She rushed over and peered at the back two tires. Nothing was wrong. The front passenger, fine as well. The driver's... and, her tire was completely shot, sagging over the rims. She wondered for a fleeting moment about how in the world Blaine had noticed that minute detail, and assumed that her car was on the way to his own parking space, and some people just noticed cars and tires, things of that nature. She supposed that Blaine was too urbane to offer to help change the thing. Still, there weren't any rocks or nails around that she could see... No construction nearby to leave random tire-piercing objects lying around...

God forbid, he might sully his starched shirtsleeves or get grime under his smooth, half-moon fingernails. He was probably even waiting there to give her a ride, since he saw that her tire was in such bad condition. Who knows how long he might have been waiting?

That is kind of nice of him, she thought, correcting the harsh judgments that she had carried of him all this time, raising her estimates ever so slightly. She would ask him to drop her off at the coffee shop three blocks down from her apartment. He'd never know the difference. After this day, she needed caffeine anyway.

Blaine's car was yellow and immaculate and sporty. Maddy couldn't see the make and model as he whisked her into the passenger's side, and honestly, she wasn't too perked about such things anyway. Yet, she did have enough layman knowledge to know that convertibles were generally more expensive than sedans. She wondered how he paid for such a vehicle, guessing that they both got approximately the same salary.

Blaine, however proud of his catch, couldn't help but notice her dingy, dusty loafers on top of his freshly vacuumed carpeting.

chapter 7

SIMON BLAZED INTO his favorite coffee haunt after finishing up his degrading shopping adventure. Four full paper sacks in hand, two in each decently muscled arm, he made his way to the counter. After all those late night stressful talks with George these past few months, he'd discovered that working out at the gym a few blocks from his apartment really helped him let off some steam. He hadn't ever been the athletic type in school, but it did help him to force his mind to stop churning on about his problems and blindly count reps.

"Chocolate-vanilla cappuccino, large, three shots," he reflexively told the pockmarked teenager behind the counter. The Coffee Cup emblemed apron seemed to be falling off of the boy, despite it being tied as tightly as it could be, the strings wound twice around his small frame.

Peering at the framed menu behind him, his eyes scrolling, the boy looked confused. He was obviously new. Even as Simon was a frequent customer, there was no way to get on too familiar terms with all the different workers, different shifts. The city was just too big.

In between this conversation, Simon waved back to the morning girl he recognized. She must be working overtime, he thought. He had long ago noted the modest yellow gold solitaire ring and its matching band on her left ring finger.

"Oh, sorry," Simon countered to the guy, "A vanilla cappuccino, three shots, add a bit of hot cocoa mix."

"To the coffee?" the cashier countered.

"Yes, please. To the coffee. Thanks."

"So you want a shot of mocha in that?" This guy didn't quit.

"No, just some cocoa, thanks."

"Mocha is chocolate. It's the same thing."

"No, it's not, but thanks anyway."

Simon tried to use his facial expression in such a way that said that he meant business, although this tactic never, ever seemed to work for him. He just had a gullible-looking face, he theorized. Whatever happened to "the customer is always right" and all of that stuff? Gone the way of the vinyl record, Simon supposed, forgotten by the masses and cherished by select connoisseurs.

"Chocolate is chocolate."

The guy shrugged, though continued to stare on. Simon couldn't help himself.

"No, actually, the chocolate – or 'mocha' – syrup that this coffee shop uses contains a large percentage of GMO corn syrup and blobs of unspecified 'artificial chocolate flavors' whereas the powder used for hot chocolate has a harder punch of purer, organic powdered cocoa and raw cane sugar."

There. This should end it. As if to add insult to injury, the guy added up the order, charged him for a hot cocoa and a cappuccino, and started to reach for the mocha syrup. Unbelievable. Simon had started to explain the virtues of The Coffee Cup's virtuous choice of using vanilla extract in their crafted beverages instead of artificially flavored vanilla-like corn juice, but the kid had stopped listening.

Just in time, like a super heroine from a comic book, the coffee girl Simon knew swooped in and took over the job, saving his paper mug from annihilation. She even gave him his dollar-something back for the hot cocoa charge, in cash though he had used a credit card. She winked at him in a non-flirtatious, "Ah, kids these days!" sort of way. Why were all the good ones married?

Instead of making him feel better, that kind act had just succeeded in making Simon feel older. He still had not gotten used to this feeling... Not being the "kid" of the "these days" that people shrugged about... not in the negative, numb way that they had just witnessed, but in that sleek, rebellious, Billy Idol-esque, wanna listen to loud music and consider getting an earring kind of way. Now, listening to loud music wasn't wild at all... fun, spontaneity, silliness wasn't rebellious.

Rebelliousness had moved closer to something grotesque, something darker and unnamed. "Rebellious" was listening to music about casually killing or raping someone. He wanted to jump into the past sometimes, but knew he couldn't. Maybe that was why some people determined – consciously or unconsciously – to never change their clothes, but to stay stuck in one certain era.

Maybe it wasn't that they weren't aware of the times, but that that simple act was their way of fighting the badness they saw in the present. Simon was much more of a fighter than that. He believed in taking the good from the bad, not leaving both to their own devices.

And all of this philosophizing about life and art and whatnot from the maddening guy getting his order wrong. No wonder he couldn't get a worthwhile date, Simon berated himself. At least George was going to some conference this weekend. Maybe it would be good for George, get his mind on other things besides Emily.

***

Maddy was sitting alone underneath a modern art canvas of an oversized coffee cup brimming with froth and coffee-related adjectives spilling out in a stamped, vintage typewriter font – hot, steaming, roasted – contemplating how nice it was that Blaine had seemed so reluctant to drop her off. Admittedly, it fueled her ego, even as she had no intention on rewarding his hesitancy or delicately pleading eyes.

Right when she noticed that the word "caffeine" is not an adjective and therefore did not fit into the theme of the painting and was reaching in her pocket for her phone to check the time, she felt a jolt of shock as her elbow was involuntarily rocked and wet heat slathered across her chest.

***

While Simon was thinking upon these things, waiting at the bar for his difficult-to-obtain cappuccino, he saw the unthinkable: *She* walked into the room… The girl from the coffee aisle at Super-Mart! One of his paper sacks tore from his tightening, sweating grip. He set them all down on the shiny cement floor to avoid further disaster.

She didn't notice him in the store; why would she notice him now? She probably wouldn't even remember him. Why should she? You can't remember someone you don't have a memory of in the first place. It was a good enough opening line though – "Oh, hey, just saw you in the grocery store a minute ago."

Acting without fully deciding, he walked over and tried it, leaving his sacks unprotected from any grocery robbers that might be lurking around, taking a coffee break.

"Hey there, so which flavor did you decide on" was what he started to say.

What he ended up saying was, "Hey...!" as he tripped on the thickly braided leather tote strap in a coiled knot in front of him, peering out from beneath the bar stool two stools away from his own.

He toppled to the ground, instinctively reaching out his hands and grasping the arm of the shocked owner of the tote. Her coffee went flying and landed on her extremely crisp, extremely white button-up shirt.

The Super-Mart girl politely did not react to his violent display of clumsiness, quietly going to sit down at the booth in the corner already occupied with her painstakingly stylish group of friends. A sea of waving hands warmly greeted her, most heavy-laden with cocktail rings. They all hugged each other before she sat down in the empty place evidently reserved for her arrival.

"Why do girls always do that, like they haven't seen each other in ages and ages?" Simon asked himself as he started the trek up and into the eyes of his splattered victim.

He could feel his cheeks swelling into hot scarlet. Her eyes were gray-green, very striking. That's all he could see at first. She was talking to him, but his embarrassment barred him from hearing.

"Oh, I'm so sorry!" He hoped he hadn't interrupted her justified tirade at him. He had, but she didn't seem to care. Silence.

"Um, let me get you a new shirt! Give you the cash for it, I mean."

She considered his offer. Maddy knew that she had three shirts basically just like this at home. She knew that she needed to branch out and wear different colors, at least. She had already been thinking about that fact.

"No, really, don't worry about it. It's just a sign that I need a new shirt," she concluded, ending the conversation with her eyes. Simon nervously pursued his lips, opening his arms to say more.

"No harm done," Maddy added, reassuringly.

Simon opened his wallet.

"No, really, it's definitely a sign. I need a new shirt anyway. I was just thinking about it." She knew at once that she had accidentally said too much and that this would serve to forward their conversation. Even though her job was to talk with strangers , dealing with them in her personal life always threw her off balance. Especially trying to talk to men. Honestly, she would have been happier if he had simply spilled the coffee on her and run out the door, avoiding this exchange altogether.

"So, that means I'm a part of the sign, then, too?" Simon mentally slapped himself for saying something so contrived-sounding.

"What?"

"Since it's a sign that you need a new shirt, therefore, I'm an acting participant in the sign-making and so it is also a sign that we're talking. See?" He knew he was making no sense and she wasted no time in telling him so.

"Nevermind. Ah... at least let me pay for the shirt to clear my own conscience."

"Sure, fine, okay."

Maddy held out her hand and Simon blindly reached into his wallet and handed her the only cash he was carrying... a ten-dollar bill. When she looked at it, she genuinely didn't mean to, but she let out a small, stifled giggle.

"What?"

"This will get the dry cleaning cost. Thank you." She caught herself. He was obviously offended, restarting the wallet search.

"All I have are cards. I can find an ATM," he offered.

"No, really, it's fine. Thank you. I've just had a rough day. Thanks."

Don't say "thanks" again, Maddy! He hadn't done anything this thankworthy, she coached herself. It didn't help. Another one just popped out.

"Thank you, sir, really."

"Sir? I'm not old enough to be a sir. But, thank you." Will the insults never end?

"Thank you. Okay. This is done. We're both just going to keep saying 'thank you' over and over."

"Yes, you're right. Bye. Nice meeting you." They shook hands and smiled awkward smiles.

***

As Maddy meandered back to her apartment from The Coffee Cup, less-than-half-full latte in hand, she realized how beautiful the street really was. Beautiful in a nontraditional sense, in a lived-in, worn-in sort of way. The colors of the city... lots of cement grays with vivid splashes of the population's personality mixed in unpredictably. She could see abandoned patches of dirt around symmetrically-placed trees, a moat of dusty brown surrounded by sidewalk, just begging to be filled with flowers again.

Dried up roots in the shape of supermarket planters were tethered between a wad of paper and an unidentifiable glass bottle, chewing gum stuck to the wavering arms of the root on one side. Someone had tried, once, and been hindered by the very nature of this place.

She opened her apartment door to the sound of nothing. Turned on all the lights. Sometimes it struck her how much she wished that things would move around a bit, be in a different place when she got home. The forest green chenille couch pillows and matching fringed throw were in exactly the same bundle Maddy had left them in last night and the black and white Bogart movie she had fallen asleep to was still lodged in the DVD player.

Maddy opened a window to let in some sound at least. A cab honked. Someone yelled. She couldn't make out what they said, which was probably not an altogether bad thing, she mused to herself.

In casual conversations, people who evidently had nothing else to say to her sad, pathetic confessions would remark about how nice it must be to not have roommates to go through your stuff or leave dishes in the sink. She always appeared happy to hear this, like it was some new revelation. "Certainly is," Maddy would confidently remark, lying through her teeth.

Even a break-in would be some sign of life. What a depressing thought. Well, she had nothing worth stealing, only the cheapest electronic gadgetry one needed for basic entertainment available along with other staple products. Oh to come home to the lights being on. Something cooking, maybe. That's reserved only for childhood and the few lucky domestics, she consoled herself.

Maybe, she thought, I'll get a contraband pet of some sort... keep it immaculately clean so that the landlord would never suspect. She'd look for articles online about what was quiet and easy to keep clean after she consulted her inbox, probably empty save for advertisements and newsletters. Rats and mice out of the question and hamsters or gerbils are too rodent-y, Maddy pondered, but guinea pigs were sort of cute, though.

Maybe she really should have invited Blaine over, he had acted so pained when she let him off. Maybe he would be interesting to be friends with... Another journalist who understood... Wait! What was she thinking? No, that would never do, she corrected herself, he's not a trustworthy sort.

She tried to jettison him from her thoughts, unsuccessfully, due to mainly the chiseled muscles pushing at the fabric of his tee shirt. And, besides, she added to her own mental list of cons against Blaine, she did not trust him (or herself) enough to put herself in that kind of a situation again. Things never worked out for her as far as relationships went. She didn't want something like that now. She wanted to know herself better and know what she wanted to get out of life before trying to get to know someone else intimately.

Yet, would it really hurt just to be friends? He would never understand that, though, she realized. No man ever just wanted to be friends unless he was at least twenty years her senior. And even then she never felt completely comfortable.

It did attract her that Blaine was completely in opposition to everything her one-time fiancé had been... After college graduation, she had said yes to Bill Howard, the only person she had dated more than a handful of times while at Indiana University. Bill was nice and wholesome and her parents had adored him. They were furious at her for breaking it off, even though they had never officially sealed the engagement with a ring. He had tried to once, but she wouldn't accept it.

Bill had told her that his grandmother had given him her mother's engagement ring for Maddy. That part thrilled her. What didn't thrill her was the fact that he had already made arrangements to melt it down to make for a grander-styled one for her with more pave diamonds that he was sure that she would love.

That told her that Bill didn't know her at all. She couldn't marry someone with that kind of unsentimental heart. She was serious on the surface, as was he, but she had thought that he had something deeper underneath it all, as did she. He was not the man to find it, evidently. Maybe he didn't have the time to yet or maybe he just didn't want to.

She had Googled him once a few years after everything had ended. It was easy to see which of the many listings with the bolded search results for "Bill Howard" that he was; the photo that came up, pointing to the homepage of his law practice, had told everything. Bill had become a moderately successful lawyer, married to someone with a normal name that she couldn't remember now.

He had the same eyes, same expression, and, predictably, less hair. But, what hair that he did still have was struggling to stay shaped into the exact same hairstyle that it was when they were in college. His wife looked like a pretty, yet normal, person... just like her name. Their "About Us" page was nothing remarkable.

They were probably happy. She hoped that they were. And, almost more than that, she hoped that the woman had insisted on a new engagement ring and that Bill had not melted down that beautiful heirloom of his great-grandmother's.

Blaine was not plain, serious, and studious as Bill had been... unrelentingly so. Blaine was extravagant, brazen, and well-dressed in his ironed, pleated ensembles. Maddy pictured him in light oranges, light mauves, or colorful prints versus Bill's diluted solid colors and reliable plaids without much distinction between colors.

Also, Blaine was confident. Maybe too much so, yes, but that seemed better to Maddy than having no confidence at all. Perhaps he was one of those people who were really very shy beneath their exteriors and their shyness made them seem haughty when they really weren't. Like herself.

If he talked to her again tomorrow, she decided that she would seriously consider giving him a chance. She was an adult now, after all. She could certainly handle things on her own.

chapter 8

GEORGE'S BRIEFCASE MADE a heavy thumping sound as it crashed onto his couch, scuffing the leather a little bit. He hadn't meant to throw it quite that hard, but, admittedly, it did feel pretty good. Got a little tension out of his system. Sometimes he felt too tired to even try to let off steam. He simply let it sit there in his brain, heated and heavy, until it eventually turned to wet vapors and then evaporated into nothingness. He was glad that he had decided not to go to that conference after all.

He usually enjoyed the longer commute from the city to his secluded country home, watching the city lights and sounds escape into the freeing landscape after a hard day's work. As his Volvo was in the shop for some minor repairs, Simon had been kind enough to give him a lift home, but they didn't talk much, having already exhausted the conversation topic most on the tip of George's mind.

Today's drive seemed to go on and on and on, even with Simon along. They mostly listened to talk radio, making mild comments about the news, neither of them very committed for or against the issues the host was addressing.

When did it become so difficult to have a conversation with one's oldest, closest friend? Every little thing seemed to remind him of Emily – their past, their present, and wondering if they had a future ahead of them.

Divorce seemed like such a depressing, thrashing word. Emily had never brought it up, and George intended never to be the one to succumb to that ever-increasing temptation. Life wasn't supposed to be easy; nobody ever claimed that it would be. He intended to fight until, well, until there wasn't anything left to fight for.

People accidentally grow apart from each other every day, George assured himself. He and Emily would simply have to identify this fact together and make a decision to get closer. He was sure that she would. Emily must not realize how meanly she has been treating him. Like Simon, the ever-literary one, had reminded him, "Identifying the problem is half of solving it."

The problem with this plan was that there didn't seem to be anything left to fight for right now, but George knew there was. He knew Simon thought he was crazy, but maybe somewhere, buried deep inside of this newer, sleeker, meaner Emily was the sweet, naïve girl that he initially married. The girl who told him that he was the one for her and that they were going to be happy together... forever.

Sometimes George felt like that she had made it all up – especially, for instance, whenever Simon unintentionally insulted George's intelligence in marrying Emily in the first place, insisting that she had always been "eerie." George continued to force himself into believing that it wasn't really that complicated, that this was normal, but then he always quickly scolded himself.

"Normal is always the enemy of great." Another Simonism. Did Simon make that one up or did some old sage say it, George pondered. Sometimes George thought that Simon used his literary image to secretly promote Simon's own ideas, letting them nonchalantly ride on the back of the prior maxims that he had spouted off from others with more intellectual clout than himself.

Though it did tend to get on his nerves when Simon quoted like that, making George feel that somehow by his quoting that Simon was demeaning the problem at hand, George knew him better than that. Simon had been that way as long as George could remember.

Simon had entered into college with a mind jam-packed with everything from witty Shakespearian quips to old adages to famous movie quotes that made absolutely no sense out of context. College literature courses had made him even wordier, however good or bad that was.

Literature was, it seemed to George, Simon's security blanket against life. It was simply his way of dealing with problems. By searching out wisdom from the greatest minds spanning centuries and centuries, quotations were the cream-of-the-crop in the way of the "right thing to say." Simon's shyness was often overcome a great deal by enabling himself to quote. Or, to talk about books when a conversation lagged. Or, to escape problems by reading entirely too much.

Simon had also done theatre in college, giving him the added advantage of saying someone else's lines. That had been good for him. Yet now, when George needed Simon to help him through this tough time, it was becoming more a source of annoyance than the endearing quality it had been.

He shut the plantation shades on his ever-darkening yard. No moon out yet. Only a satellite pretending to be a star on the navy horizon.

George didn't know what his "security blanket" was. Must he know what it is in order to remove it from his life and start anew? Couldn't he just remove everything and hope that it, whatever it was, was caught up in the hasty clean sweep?

Again, George wished that he had the confidence that Simon had to bring up some usually-obscure conversation topic like that, diving into it in great detail, and automatically thinking that everyone else in the room either is or should be interested in whatever he's talking about. If Simon finds a topic interesting and has confidence in its aesthetics, he has no qualms in trying to rile up other people to be passionate about it as well.

Conversely, Simon had always bragged about George's ability to make people talk about themselves. Yet, George felt that the magnet he held up for people – complete strangers, sometimes – to vent his or her life story to him wasn't an ability. A gift maybe, but not a skill or ability.

Superficial subject matters, those about movies and books and such, were what was required in easy conversation... Not deep psychological probing. Nothing pressing. That's what he and Emily lacked, he decided. Good, but only very lightly stimulating, conversation. If they spoke at all for more than a few scattered and meaningless sentences, they could only seem to talk about miserably heavy things.

This kind of thinking was getting him nowhere.

He knew that he was going in circles, the same familiar circles he wound himself in when he worried over his fading marriage. Rubbing the little scuff on the couch and making it appear less noticeable with the oils in his fingertips, he decided that taking a nap might be a worthwhile idea. Just kill all the thoughts at once instead of attempting to unravel them.

Suddenly at that very thought, as if on cue, a huge wave of exhaustion crept over him. George sunk into the couch, neatly leaned up his briefcase against the immaculately polished coffee table beside him, and called out into the dim emptiness for Darby, who came chattering into the room.

To George's mild astonishment, Darby actually came to him and happily curled up in a ball on his lap. One never could tell with this little guy, whether or not he'd choose to be a friend or fiend at any given moment. A lot of the time they were on more friendly terms when Darby's "real" master – or rather mistress – was out of the house.

Sleep instantly wrapped its strong arms around George and he was gone, Darby snoring away peaceably on his chest, half under and half on top of the suit jacket he had been too preoccupied to take off.

***

"Whoohoooo!"

Emily giddily yelled out of the open convertible top of a yellow sports car as it sped down the curvy highways of the New York countryside, her arms surfing the hard breeze. The wall of wind felt like it could be strong enough to bruise her chest and arms. She loved feeling the wind's strength against her, loved how it seemed to want to free her from her shirt, pulling the thin cloth off her back with all of its fingerless might. Her lover was clinging to her naked, skirted leg as he drove, his eager fingertips riding higher with each passing moment.

"Max, honey, are you drivin' or trying to get something you're just gonna get later now?! Both hands on!"

The driver angrily skidded his hand away, grabbing the steering wheel with both hands and pushing the gas pedal harder. Instantly, Emily regretted this last order she'd given. Max had such masculine hands, but not at all rough or calloused...

"I didn't say both hands on the wheel, now did I? Make a decision!"

The car screeched to a halt. The ignition and lights turned off in a flash. Max forcibly pulled Emily down from her perch gripping the windshield with her fingertips and hoisted her into the backseat, flinging a couple of empty glass bottles out of the way. Her arms made crinkly noises as she scooted backward onto the paper sacks that the bottles had been wrapped in.

Emily's wild laughter unashamedly, unabashedly echoed down the empty street as Max stood in the open car door, swiftly dealing with zippers, buttons. Twice a pair of headlights illumed their bodies; each time the passing was car going too fast to notice their car resting in the tree-shaded shoulder.

***

George did not stir when Emily casually reached over and unlocked the deadbolt from the nest of her muscled lover's arms, he then hoisting her over the threshold like a cruel mocking of the time-honored newlywed ritual. He only drowsily opened his eyes as Darby barked his usual short, snappy greeting to Emily and jumped off of his lap, using George's body as a platform to catapult himself over the top of the couch and onto the gray-white marble tiled floor.

Since Darby did not bark up a storm, as he always did when strangers came to the house, George had no way of preparing for what he saw displayed before him. And, since his car was not parked in its customary place in the driveway, neither did Emily and Max.

Even if George had of had a moment or two to limber up his tightened thoughts to accept this concrete blow, it wouldn't have helped. The parties exchanged glances, each shooting through the other with a million different words, a million different worries.

***

Simon couldn't help it. He had thought about her all that day and all the next. She wasn't like an ordinary unmemorable stranger, one of the hundreds of faces that he unconsciously took in every day. Even after time had passed, her features did not blend in to the overall atmospheric makeup of the city like most people he met in passing seemed to do, making her into sort of a vague blur of a memory that escaped him.

Everything about her was still very clearly in his mind. The irony, he thought, was that he could not remember the face of the Super-Mart girl who had directed his attention to Madeline Bryson in the first place.

So, decidedly, Simon took a jump. He heard the dial tone in his ear and waited patiently, feeling foolish and childish and any number of things, debating whether to simply hang up or not. No, because then she might call back questioningly since his number would be in her phone's missed calls list. Then she'd think he was a coward. What if he...

Cutting off his racing thoughts, she answered easily. Though she didn't recognize the number, she automatically thought that it must be one of the copy editors asking her a quick question about an article.

"Hello?"

"Ah... Hi. Is this, um... Madeline R. Bryson?"

"Yes, it is."

Jessica D. Lovett

Yes! Simon remembered that that was indeed her voice and knew he had just one shot at this. *Wow, she really has a compelling voice, strong but feminine*, Simon thought.

"Um...."

Blasted hesitation! He tried again, pushing the words out, mustering all the strength of his faculties.

"Are you the beautiful woman I spilled coffee on yesterday?"

Silence. It sounded like Maddy accidentally laughed a little, quickly shielding the phone with her hand. Simon chose interpret the lingering silence as a question.

"Well, see, a calling card fell out of your purse or maybe your pocket or something, and I didn't know whether it was your own or whether it was a colleague or a business contact or friend of yours or something like that, but then I thought I might call to see if it were possibly your own personal business card and I could talk to you again or something."

Stupid. Stupid. Stupid. Simon moaned inside. How many times had he said the word "something" in those brawling sentences? He just knew he had just blown it completely.

"I believe so, yes."

"Yes?"

"Yes, that it was me that you spilled coffee on." She was having fun with this.

"Oh, well, great. Well, not GREAT that I spilled it on you, I mean. 'Great' that, well... Ah... You know..."

"So, is that Miss Bryson or Mrs. Bryson? Or, Mrs. Something Else, as in not taking your husband's name or something, which is perfectly fine..."

He'd done it again, twice! Why did he keep saying that, Simon reprimanded himself, determined not to let the dreaded "something" creep into their conversation again.

"Skip it. It's okay, really," Maddy saved. "How about tomorrow night?"

"Great!" Simon countered, sighing and wondering how it had been so simple.

"Great. Then, see you tomorrow."

"Tomorrow it is!"

They both hung up. Smiled. And, then tried calling each other back when they realized, almost simultaneously, that they hadn't decided when, where, or what tomorrow would hold. After the first few tries of being directed to each other's voice-mail, since they were both calling at once, they finally stopped playing phone tag, laughingly discussed the matter, and decided to meet back at The Coffee Cup at six, after Maddy got off work.

***

As Emily nervously bit down on her lip, she tasted traces of saltiness. Sweat still clung to her brow, making a few stray hairs stick to her freshly reapplied lipstick. Using her free hand to try and put them back into place, she smelled Max's crisp cologne melded in to her own skin. Guilt was permeating her from the inside, evidences of her guilt written on her every pore.

There was no escaping it. No way to explain it away this time. She had been out all night and that was that. There was nothing to say to one another, so she said nothing. At least George was at that conference. She wasn't ready to say goodbye to Max yet. He'd been to the house plenty of times during the day, but now... The dark of night fell over them both and seemed

Jessica D. Lovett

to seal the deal. Max was hers. Finally she'd found a man who was fun, who took risks, who gave her what she needed...

She and Max had been laughing so full-heartedly that upon opening the door, and unexpectedly seeing George there, it was as if emotional brakes were applied to the laughter, full force, but that the physical act of laughter was so strong that it could not be stopped right away. She still heard it in her mind and fought it down as it stubbornly died away with the painful silences that emerged, even as nothing was funny to her anymore. Adrenaline shot through all three of them, making them ache in tandem with each other, unawares.

***

George couldn't move at all and had no desire to. Maybe, he felt, if he stayed locked into place as hard as he could, this moment would melt away and he would allow himself room to wake up from this terrible nightmare. Any sudden movement might thrust him into this reality, banishing the aspect of its being a removable night terror. Having the least emotional ties to the situation, Max spoke first.

"Maxwell... Blaine Maxwell."

He dried his palm on his slacks and stuck his hand out to George. George looked at the hand like it was a separate part of this Max guy - a severed, random hand that had no owner to speak of. He explored it with his eyes, this hand that had stolen his life from him, and made no move toward or against it.

George's thought process was that if he were having a night terror, there would be no negative consequences for his actions. He found himself manically grabbing on to this threadbare mentality, as a half-starved wild creature grabs onto some helpless prey, though, in another more logical state he would've realized its fallacy. With swiftness he didn't know he still had, George leaped in a single bound up and over the couch. Both fists began swinging with all his might, and some added strength he didn't know he had ever had, at the smarmy face connected with the smarmy hand that was just offered to him.

He had no idea that something as despicable to him as violence could feel so good. George's right knuckles smashed Max in the lips... the lips that Max had touched his wife with. George found himself lapsing into Shakespeare's "Macbeth" for some unknown reason, perhaps simply the violent essence of the thing, an essence unfamiliar to him except in the context of literature.

"Out!" he desperately screamed, in an uncontrollable voice not his own.

George recoiled, his fingers throbbing from the powerful hit and damp with Max's saliva. He didn't think, just went back at Max again, this time with the left fist raised and pulled back behind his head to gather as much force as humanly possible. Max teetered back, shocked. George's business executive's hands making contact with Max's sharp teeth made blood rise from small tears in George's thin flesh. George wiped the blood off of the top of his hand and onto his pants in one quick motion, yelling again, with all of his might, "Out!"

This time, Max was ready. He pulled back and jerked to the corner of the pastel-colored room, his face making a collage with the gigantic, grandiose silk flower arrangement on the small table in the corner. Max scoured the room for something in George's own home, of his personal belongings, to be warped and used against him as a makeshift weapon.

Having the advantage of being more familiar with the terrain, George had been ready for this, his primal fighter's instinct resurrected lightning-fast from a previously unknown place inside. Darby's heavy wrought-iron dog chaise gained momentum as it hurled through the air and George thundered, "Damned!"

Dark bruises began to form on the surface of George's skin. He didn't stop to notice them. He kept going despite injury and despite his better judgments, now fully aware that he was not conjuring this scene in his sleep. Then, George lost track of what he was doing, how many times he had hit and been hit, been kicked and kicked back. All was a wall of fists, arms, feet, skulls, elbows, and pieces of his home being hurled at him before he could think to prepare or cover his face.

George's only mistake was in locking eyes with Emily. When George had turned around and had seen her watching this all unfold, years of damage manifesting in only a matter of seconds, he had seen a single tear falling from her eyes. After he stared for a moment, he spied several more tears blending on her cheeks. She never, ever cried and it had taken him aback.

Was she crying for him, or for Max, or for their marriage ending, or for the affair's end, or just to cruelly distract him, or for what?

These conflicting thoughts were so large in his mind that they gave George pause… just the pause that Max needed to intercept George's next blow and forfeit his intended final yell of "Spot, I say!"

***

"So, should I have told you I'd be the guy with a yellow carnation or will you recognize me?" Simon chatted with Madeline on the phone. Her number was already programmed into his cell. Just in case she called him, he wanted to be prepared by seeing her name pop up on the caller ID panel and therefore not sound flustered or surprised to hear her voice on the line. Calm, cool, and collected. That was his goal.

"I'll recognize you."

"How can you be sure?"

"It was just yesterday, you know..."

***

When Maddy got to the coffee shop, she spotted him instantly. He was sitting on an exotic patterned couch in the corner, touting a yellow carnation and a silly, mock-charming grin. She had to laugh, having thought that he was just trying to be funny on the phone by referencing all those old movies with mysterious first meetings and the guy holding a certain pre-agreed upon flower to be recognized only by the girl he was meeting there. And, here he was really holding one!

She saw how he was trying to be funny in both ways – with the reference to over-the-top vintage romantic comedies and the actual presence of the flower both, playing off each other – the visual irony that caught Maddy so off guard being the clench of it, clearly exhibiting Simon's offbeat sense of humor. As Maddy walked closer and closer to him, she felt heat rising to her face and hoped that she wasn't blushing. She loved black and white movies... How could he know that?

Her mind began to chastise her, analyzing the situation more than necessary. Why had she said yes to Simon so easily? And, in the circumstances of his call! Did she want him to think that she was easy? Why did even she say yes in the first place? She never said yes to anyone! What was she thinking? And saying yes to someone that would brazenly call a girl from an intentionally left-behind business card? She would have to be honest about that someday. That she had let it fall out of her purse to test him.

Maddy had, admittedly, laughed at his joke about being grateful that she had "dropped" her name so graciously, referring to her dropping her card onto the floor. She liked his carefree manner... And, yet...

Now, Blaine would think she was dating someone and not ask her out. He would be sure and know; The Coffee Cup was where everyone came after work. Oh, who cares about such a preening peacock like Blaine anyway? "Why can't I ever just enjoy the moment?" she chided herself, determined to stop the stream of bothersome thoughts before she got close enough to Simon for him to read her expression and misinterpret the worried undertones that were undoubtedly surfacing upon her face.

chapter 9

FA...

　　...LL...

　　　　ING...

As George gave in to the hardness of the floor, he found a kind of relief after deep, reverberating waves of pain ran into the horizontal wall he was facing and was allowed to finish its task. He had stopped fighting the pulsing agony but wasn't sure when or why. The ground had touched him, feverishly rising up to meet him, and now he couldn't move. All that was within him had been mercilessly silenced before he was ready. As if he could ever be ready.

With this free reign he'd given it, the pain began to grow, living and breathing as if it were another entity entirely mastering his body. The sharpness of the pain melded into a muffled bruise, perceivable only in blunt ways, spreading throughout all George's limbs instead of merely being limited to the point of the pain's origin.

First, he saw an excruciatingly brilliant flash of white light swallow up the world around him. After it passed, there was a dark circle around his eyes – no, around his eyesight. It was a hideous circle (or were there two circles?) and both eyes could see only through them, as though he were looking through a pair of furry binoculars.

Was he awake or asleep? How could he tell? The focus of George's gaze began to lengthen, in tandem with the pain in his head or neck or shoulder or wherever it was. After a moment, the tiny, round windows of vision coexisting with the blackness became smaller, and smaller, and smaller, until… it stopped and he could see and hear nothing. There was nothing left to see or hear. Nothing. Anywhere.

The world moved on without George Morris for a time. His spirit and mind traveled elsewhere, absent from the moments that followed.

His wounds, however, continued to live on. Most of the blood that trickled down instantly sank in to the wrinkle-free fabric of his suit, disappearing into the dark, textured navy cloth as if its deep red tones had never existed. Any red flecks on his white Oxford shirt cowered beneath his jacket and loosened maroon tie. From far away, the tie looked like a river of blood itself, coursing onto the otherwise pristine floor and mysteriously stopping at a point.

***

Max stared at George's lifeless form for a moment, meticulously accessing the damage he had inflicted upon it. He wondered, for a brief moment, if he had gone too far, and if so, what would he do with the corpse?

Thankfully, as Max starred it down, he detected that the buttons on the speckled white shirt began to move slightly, slowly, as George's lungs desperately warred with the rest of him to keep on going.

***

George's weighted-down mind tried to catch up and failed, over and over. He thought that he heard instructions reading out loud in his head, like the talking warning signs in the London underground.

Keep breathing. In and out. In and...

...Out.

Keep pumping blood. However much is lost in the effort. Keep. On.

But, why? He asked himself this. Fed these words into his own mind. The warning words stopped. Paused. And started up again, after considering his question.

KEEP ON.

The few words that Max and Emily began to exchange bounced in and out of George's ears, some being received by his mind in a jumbled, mangled kind of way while others were lost completely to the stale, acidic air.

"Pitiful. He couldn't even get that part right," Max huffed.

"What? What are you..." Emily started to ask, but was interrupted.

"The quote from 'Macbeth' he launched into so dramatically."

"When?" Emily was genuinely curious.

"What he was yelling? When we were fighting?"

"Yeah..."

"The 'Out! Out!' and all that?" Max added, reprovingly.

Emily indicated that she understood, or at least wanted to communicate that she understood whether she actually did or not, with a slow nod.

"The correct quotation from Act 5, Scene 1 would be 'Out, damn'd spot! out, I say!' and not 'Out! Out! Damned spot,' adding the 'I say' at the end, as I'm sure your husband was planning to say. Putting the two out's together? It's a common mistake. It's misquoted in popular culture all the time. Evolved into being accepted that way..."

Emily was looking through Max, unhearing. Looking astonished, as if he had just made some profound point. Who knew Max knew Shakespeare? He kept going. Emily kept, obviously, not hearing him but looking as though she was intensely interested. What interested her more was the fact that Max and George could both quote the same book, whatever it was. She had pushed them so far apart from one another in her mind that she was slightly offended by this revelation.

At this, George retreated back into his mind. The words were too much, too many for him to read with his mind's eye.

He realized that his taste buds were inundated by salt. He couldn't get it to go away. He thought about it, thought *at* it, like maybe that would do something, be an action itself, but nothing happened.

He thought that he moved once, but was wrong. All movement was captured.

***

Emily's rolling eyes punctuated Max's speech, quickly reeling it in to a close.

"Well, I am a journalist. Don't you think that I took literature courses?"

"Wull, I did, too! Woop-de-do!" Emily countered, hands leaping to clasp her hips. There was a pause. Longer than it should be.

"Well, good." Max shrugged and paused yet again before choosing to continue. "I just happened to really like 'Macbeth' when we read it in my sophomore Brit. Lit. class."

Max could tell that his forced apologetic tone made Emily feel superior, just the way she wanted to feel. He knew just how to mold a situation to suit her needs so that his could be met later. Blaine Maxwell was a patient man... patient to a point, that is.

All this trouble, and his hand was beginning to show a bruise a little bit, too, all for what? He found himself gazing at her photo over the mantle, arm gently resting on George's suited, as usual, shoulder. Max shot his eyes away, suddenly disgusted, but not sure why.

***

This was embarrassing. People were looking at them and grinning. She could feel them saying, "Awww... what a cute couple. Isn't that sweet?" Maddy shuddered. Being conspicuous was not usually an objective of hers. But, in another way, she didn't care.

Simon was fun. And, handsome. Very. Yet, not in a traditional way. Almost all of his appeal was all locked up in his eyes. Without paying attention to those eyes, he might pass for just a normal, everyday, average guy. She didn't mind if people thought that she, for once, had an attractive *and* funny boyfriend. Let 'em talk. She'd never had had a reason for them to before.

He didn't seem to notice the stares, or, if he did, he paid them no mind. Without warning, Simon froze.

"Wait, I just had an idea!"

"For what?"

Jessica D. Lovett

"Ummm... you're going to have to learn the truth sooner or later. I'm trying to write. Please don't run away," Simon teased, squinting his eyes and his smile simultaneously. "And, don't laugh either!"

Maddy laughed.

"Madeline, I just asked you kindly not to laugh!"

"Sorry! Couldn't help it. Forgive me," she begged dramatically, hands clasped, completely out of her character. She had no idea what had come over her, but she liked it. The kids used to pick on her for being so serious all the time. A stick in the mud.

Additionally, Maddy had no idea how to flirt properly or carry on a light conversation with a man, but Simon didn't seem to notice that problem either. Goodness knows her mother had tried to teach her... "Look him in the eye a beat too long and then look away sheepishly, Maddy, let's give it a try! Show me sheepish!" her mother had coached.

"Just a sec," Simon muttered as he reached behind him into the inside pocket of his distressed brown leather jacket hanging on his chair. He grabbed out a mini yellow legal pad.

"The best!" he tipped the tattered pad in the air and started jotting with his pen, lodged on the cardboard base of the notepad. Maddy didn't know what it was, but she could tell that it was no ordinary pen... it was sleek, matte navy blue and gold and something about it perfectly fit Simon's personality, if it was possible for a pen to match someone.

He saw her staring and felt the need to apologize for its apparent price tag. Simon twirled the pen through his fingers.

"A gift from my dad. An important gesture that he supports my crazy, irrational writing fantasies."

Maddy nodded an open-ended kind of nod, letting him know that he could go on if he wished to elaborate. Old jacket, frayed and cheap notepad, expensive pen, and really expensive watch. She wondered what this said about this Simon Kincade. He looked up a couple of times, flashing a broad, sarcastic smile at the audience of Maddy's coworkers scattered at the tables surrounding them.

"Are you, ahem, making a scene, Simon?" Maddy smiled coquettishly.

"Why, Miss Madeline Bryson! You made a joke!"

"I, ah... You can call me Maddy. Most people do." Come to think of it, she mused, most people call her by her full name and not her nickname. No matter.

"I got it! You were, weren't you? I'm proud of you. 'Making a scene' with the people looking and writing this idea down, you were teasing me! Irony! I'm rubbing off on you and it's only our first date."

She couldn't manage a reply, so he continued for her. "Don't know if that's a good thing or not! What will your editor think when my brilliant musings begin to seep into your writing?"

Maddy couldn't stop her schoolgirl-esque giggling. It broke free from her and went on a rampage – relative for her at least – accumulated from all the previous jokes and just the whole awkward first date situation. Simon laughed at her and with her, both, unable to resist the childish giggles that came out of this business suit kind of girl.

"That's... ah... a bit pretentious, isn't it?" Maddy finally mustered to speak again, but with all the lilt let loose in her voice, she sounded like she was trying to talk through an intense pillow fight that she was on the losing side of.

"Maybe, but it's called flirting. Heard of it? It's this secret way of making outlandish romantic assertions like that to people that you like, without admitting you really like them, in order to gauge their reactions..." Simon looked almost like he was about to wink at her but didn't. His smile was bolstered, fortified from having had the ability to make laughter sing out of Maddy like that.

"How'd I do? How was my reaction gauged?" Almost recovered from the laughing spell, she tried to look serious, but her voice was still alight with laughter.

"I dunno yet... You're a hardcover book, Miss Maddy Bryson." There was the wink. Maddy blushed. Again. Only this time she didn't care nearly so much that she had done it.

"What's your middle name?" Maddy blurted without thinking.

"Clyde. What's yours?"

"Rose. Do you know what your name means?"

"Nope. Not sure if it means anything."

"I think name meanings are important. We'll have to look it up on a later date!" Maddy winked back, proud of her fledgling flirting skills.

"Pretty good, pretty good! I'm impressed! Good first try, Maddy..."

All at once and without either of them knowing exactly how it happened or who reached out first, Maddy and Simon were holding hands.

***

Simon walked home floating on air that night. He was so happy that he forgot to lament over not writing anything on his novel all day. How could it have been that easy? He couldn't wait to see her again in a couple of days. He'd have to think of something fun to do... not the same tired dinner and a movie routine. Maybe they'd see a movie and *then* have dinner? Blah.

Something interesting... something unique... He strained his brain for ideas. What would impress her?

"Hello, Mr. Kincade. Nice evening." The doorman greeted him as usual. "Nice evening." "Nice day." "Nice morning." Never a question. Just a flavorless statement.

"Oh, hey, Edmund! How's it going?"

Edmund Hopkins smiled and nodded unspeaking as Simon walked by, also as usual. Simon remembered that he had turned off his cell phone during their date, so he flipped it open to change it back and noticed that he had eight missed calls and three new voice messages! Looking at the list, there were two all George's office number and the rest from a number he didn't recognize. He dialed his voicemail.

"Message one. From (555) 506-9973. Sent today at five oh-eight p.m." "Simon. This is Agnes Bloom, George's secretary? Well, of course, you know who I am. Well. Call me." That's odd, Simon thought. "Message two. From (555) 646-5743. Sent today at nine fifteen p.m." "Simon. Agnes again. This is my cell. Please call me as soon as you can."

Simon's first thought was that Emily must have asked for a divorce. George must be devastated and sitting at his big desk depressed and not going home and Agnes wants me to cheer him up and take him home or to my place or something. He was sure that's what it was. He hit reply and called her cell.

"Hi, Agnes, this is Simon. Sorry it took me a while to get back with you... Ah, I'll be glad to come pick George up. I'll be at the office in a few minutes. Just got home." Silence on the other end. "Agnes?"

"Simon. Listen to me." She sounded like she was crying, fighting to stay calm. George must have signed a demon of a pre-nup for her to sound that morose.

Jessica D. Lovett

"I'm listening."

"I am not at the office."

"Well, where are you?"

"George is in ICU."

Simon dropped his cell phone and had to tell himself to lean down and pick it up again. Agnes undoubtedly heard a loud crash on her end of the line.

"Sorry. Did you say…"

"Yes. I'm here with him."

"What happened?"

Agnes paused before she spoke, waiting for the boulder of words to hit the ground

before continuing.

"He was attacked. They called me first since I was his most frequent cell contact."

"Ah! Is he okay? Has someone canceled his cards?"

"Simon, he wasn't mugged on the street. He was attacked in his home. After he went home from work. It doesn't look like they took anything."

"Where's Emily?"

"Who knows? She won't answer her phone. She is probably, you know, *out* or something…"

"Agnes!"

"Yes?"

"Where are you?"

"We're at Presbyterian."

"I'll be there… now."

Simon flipped the phone shut and jumped into the first cab he could hail, not even answering or hearing Edmund's polite "Is something wrong?" and "May I help you?" inquiries as he sped through the lobby.

chapter 10

BLAINE MAXWELL AND Emily Morris sped down the empty highway, one large bold yellow streak streaming alongside the thin yellow center stripe of the open road.

***

It is not often that Simon felt like crying. The fact was, he couldn't even remember the last time he did. Yet, if there were something that could make him show tears in a public place, this would be it. George had always been there for him though scrapes. Always. And here he was, trying to actually "be there" for George, to do something besides just listen and offer up relationship advice – not even good advice for that matter, since most of it was not first-hand experience. But, this was not a scrape. This was a fracture.

It exasperated him that there was nothing he could do physically, seeing that he was a physical, kinesthetic kind of person. He wanted action! Something! Yet, there was nothing he could do at all except sit and stare at this marred version of his best friend's face, hoping to see his eyes open so that he could frantically search for any trace of spirit left in his eyes.

Jessica D. Lovett

Would George ever be himself again? Would Simon ever hear his voice? Would anything (anything!) ever be the same again? It certainly did not look good to Simon. His mind felt slippery and he couldn't hold on to any single thoughts, just drown in the one obliterating, bruised and bleeding image in front of him.

"It's been fifteen minutes, sir," an obviously sympathetic nurse offered up to Simon.

Simon didn't move. Maybe if he ignored the guy, he would just leave Simon alone. What harm could he, could anyone, do now? What was the fifteen-minute rule for, anyway?

"I'll have to ask you to go to the main waiting room now."

"Fine. Sure."

Simon dragged his feet across the overly shiny tiles until he reached the elevator, passing through the maze of clear glass compartments of patients, mostly in medically induced sleep for the pain they were in. Neat little rectangular arrangements of suffering. His eyes were aimed down. After a little searching, he found the waiting room where Agnes said she would be waiting for him.

Agnes sat in one corner of the room in a hard gray plastic chair, in suspended animation, holding on to her cotton hand-kerchief. Simon could tell that it was quite old by the slightly yellow color of it, yet it was freshly pressed around the sweeping representation of the letters "A" and "J," with one big swirled "B" in the middle. Simon looked at the block-lettered monogram of his watch. There was something about monograms that made a person feel like a grownup. Gave you a tangible reminder you of who you are at those times when it was easy to forget.

And then there was George... wrapped up in a dingy hospital gown, nondescript, colorless, worn by who knows how many other people and probably some of them had died in that very cloth. Then again, maybe they didn't keep it if the people died. Yet, wouldn't they have to? Wouldn't that be a huge expense? Aw, hospitals always charge an arm and a leg for anything so surely they throw "extremely used up" hospital gowns away. This tidbit of skepticism consoled Simon for the moment.

He tried to shake the image of agony that his heart had latched on to so severely, tried to see George's normal, un-battered face, but he could not find it.

"Tell me again what he... um... has?" Simon's voice squeaked a little and he didn't care. Didn't try to cover it up.

Agnes began the list once more, all in one tone of voice as if she were reciting words for a spelling bee, "Cerebral edema, ruptured spleen and kidney trauma, two broken ribs, light concussion, fractured left ankle, broken right femur."

She stopped. The list was over.

"Wow. What, which, is life threatening?"

"All of it," Agnes stared ahead, not turning to look at Simon, "well, except for the breaks and the obvious hurts...." She touched her own unbruised cheek.

The thought of George's purple eyelids made Simon's own eyes ache.

"How do, you know, remember all this?"

"I asked the doctor."

Simon didn't have anything else to say, so he didn't try. Agnes didn't seem to mind. He had asked the doctor, too, but none of it had stayed with him. His thoughts had been completely full, overflowing, with the shell lying before him, slowly ripping his heart out. No other pain would fit. Simon felt numb.

"At least they were able to stop the internal bleeding. Keep him from going into shock."

Simon nodded, like he knew the ramifications of what that meant when really he just thought it sounded terrible and horrible and wanted to leave it at that.

So there they sat for the next few hours until Agnes left at around ten or so, leaving Simon alone for the rest of the night, attempting to throw their love and support at an almost lifeless body, running solely because of modern technology. Big, gray machines. Blinking lights. Florescent bulbs making their skin paler than it already was, making them look even sadder than they already were. Random beeps and the scampering feet of people in scrubs and lab coats were the dominant sounds. Every time they were allowed to visit, which was more than the rules actually admitted due to the compassion on them given by a couple of nurses, they had `rotated and went in one at a time. Agnes... then an hour... Simon... another cold hour... Agnes...

Simon couldn't help thinking how ironic it was that since he had always been mildly cynical about technology, through the years preferring the natural and organic – from acoustic music to fresh food – to the sleek and technical, and here it was, sustaining the one he loved the most nonetheless, without holding his prior prejudice against him.

The clock ticked. Its clicking combined with the beep of the IV bothered Simon, making irregular beats that clashed and kept him awake. At around midnight, he had almost accidentally drifted off during one of his shifts to visit George's room, but a random scream from down the hall had made him jump.

***

When Simon had left the building in such a rush and didn't come in that night, Edmund began to wonder what was up. Deep in his gut, he had a feeling that it involved his daughter somehow, but had no idea why or how. All he knew was that he had to find out. And fast.

***

It hadn't occurred to Simon before to ask what exactly had happened to George. Agnes had told him what the injuries were, yes, but the fact that something caused them was so foreign to him that it was almost physically painful to shove the concept into his mind. Simply the shock that it had happened was almost all that his system could take. At about half past two, several hours after Agnes had finally left, he had glanced at his watch and thought to himself that George had just talked to him on the phone at two thirty that afternoon. All had been peachy a mere twelve hours ago.

Time was not on his side... it passed too slowly when he wanted it to race past with full force and then turned around and stole moments away that he would have loved to relish, letting them roll around in his mind like melting chocolate, tasting them slowly and deliberately.

Half past two and two minutes. He didn't exactly want to know the answer, but he had to. Maybe it had just been a random burglar. Would that make it easier or harder?

"Who?"

Agnes had pretended not to know what he was talking about when he had asked her for more details, in order to put off answering. Simon didn't clarify his question, despite her best efforts to avoid it. He didn't need to. Simon replayed their conversation in his head as he went in and out of wakefulness

Jessica D. Lovett

in George's darkened hospital room. He had been shocked at Agnes's bluntness regarding Emily.

"They don't know, Simon, but that devil woman isn't here in mourning, is she?"

"She's pretty evil, yeah, but is she really capable..."

"I don't know, Simon, I just don't know. There's no love in her, none in her eyes.

I know that she didn't love our George..."

"Then why did she marry him?"

This was a question that had burned at Simon, and probably had singed George, too. No one knew the answer and perhaps they never would. Agnes offered up her theory.

"He's a nice man, comfortable to be around, easy on the eyes... Maybe she just wanted..."

"Maybe she just wanted a footstool!" Simon had snapped, ashamed at himself when he saw Agnes's eyes fall. "A *spare* footstool!"

The hatred in his heart for Emily, hatred for what she had done to George's spirit, snapped up inside the words.

"I can't stand it either. We will stand by him, though, won't we? We'll help him fix this."

While Simon wasn't exactly sure what part Agnes was intending for them to fix, he had eagerly agreed. He had gone home around three, shuffling along completely on auto-pilot. He'd almost forgotten how it felt to navigate the city without anyone bustling around him and with all baptized in darkness except for artificial light. With hardly anyone on the streets, it felt like a hollow apocalyptic movie where he was the zombie.

***

As early as he could muster, Simon went up to the hospital. Agnes had already been there for some time and the nurse told him that he had to wait for his turn. Simon hated ICU rules. *What was going to happen if two people went in there at once? And what's with the measly fifteen minutes on the hour limit? Would the patient randomly expire?* He sleepily grumbled to himself in the dull waiting room until he noticed a family had appeared in the corner and they were looking at him like he was a weirdo, causing him to realize that he'd been airing his concerns audibly.

After a couple of rotations visiting George, Agnes insisted that they both run to her home for something to eat and some tea. Simon was reluctant at first, not wanting to leave George. Deep inside of himself, Simon felt as if something terrible would happen to George if someone was not there holding on to his hand every second of the day - at least every second that was allowed in the visitation rules - pumping life into him with the blood in their own veins. He didn't want to let go, but Agnes took his hand and led him away. A soft couch did sound pretty inviting. The time that it took for them to get there passed by quickly, both of them silent and deep in thought.

As Agnes opened her front door, she excitedly spied the answering machine light blinking red into the blackness. Almost tripping over a wayward umbrella sticking out from the coat rack, she scurried over and triumphantly pressed the "Play Messages" button.

Beep. "This is a private call for James Bloom. Please call back as soon as possible at 1-800...." Judging by her expression, the computerized voice fell from Agnes's primed mind.

She sighed as she pressed delete, then pressed the message button once more, even though the new message light was not lit up.

Jessica D. Lovett

"You want to hear my precious grandbabies, Simon? Of course you do!" she asked and answered, not looking to him for a response.

"You have...ZERO...new messages and...TWO...old messages." Simon watched as Agnes mouthed the words of the two messages, holding her clasped hands to her hip. Beep. "Message two. Friday, December twenty-fifth, eleven a.m." A cheery but strained voice piped in.

"Hey, Mom! Here're the kids..." "Gra-mma! Merry Christmas!" This sounded like two boys chiming in together, a little girl voice appending with "I miss you Grandma!" taped to the end of the shouting. Then a small boy's voice again, "I love you, Graaaamma!" "Me, too!" from two voices together. Click. Beep.

"Message one. Monday, December twenty-first, three p.m." "Mom, it's me. Peter is...well, we have to change our plans. I'm so sorry to do this. Again. Call me, okay? I'm so sorry. Maybe we can...." Agnes fiddled with the machine to cut off her daughter's message.

"My daughter, Janie..." she explained to Simon, without really explaining anything. Janie had a childlike voice herself, high and feminine, but the tinged of sadness made it decidedly an adult voice.

Beep. The machine had cut off the woman's sentence, but not the meaning behind it. Simon looked up and saw a gray storm cloud in Agnes's eyes that made him want to rush over and hug her, try to bat it out of her ordinarily blue sky.

"My poor little daughter," Agnes said, not really speaking to Simon especially but just letting the words come. "Janie keeps repeating like sick mantra, 'He's getting better, he's getting bet-

112

ter, Mom, he is.' What does that mean? Cheating less? Being a nicer husband? What?"

"So many marital problems!" Simon trembled. "Why bother at all?"

"Because, Simon," Agnes brightened, "marriage can be, as it was with my darling James and I, a heavenly blessing beyond your imagining. People just don't want to put in the effort."

"I guess. But, how can you possibly find the right person?" Simon sank into the tapestry-like pictures of flower gardens woven into Agnes's couch.

"Maybe this sounds like a cliché, but you don't. You become the right person."

"Oh, Agnes…"

"Now, excuse me Simon. Make yourself at home. I've got to make a call."

"Like Shakespeare said, 'Action is eloquence.' I agree."

"Right. And, speaking of which, why don't you call up that pretty girl of yours? Get her to come over and cheer up an old lady. We'll have tea." Simon laughed at this. Agnes dialed Janie's number. "Why hello, Peter." She paused for what felt like a little too long, biting her tongue. "Let me speak to Janie. No, I don't care if she's busy. I'll wait."

But, Simon thought, not brave enough to argue with Agnes to her face, *Darling James died. That doesn't sound like a "heavenly blessing" kind of thing to me! Finally being happy, then pouf! Gone!*

Agnes put her delicate palm over the mouthpiece of the phone while she waited for Peter to get Janie. "That Peter…" she sighed. "And," as though she could hear Simon's thoughts, making him worry that maybe in his tired stupor that he'd accidently spoken them aloud, "even though James went to be with Jesus before I got to, that doesn't matter one bit. He's inside me still and I love him still and I'm sure he loves me and is waiting for me where he's at now. That's a blessing, too. No fear for the future." Janie had finally picked up and Simon went to check the kettle and such as to give Agnes a little privacy.

***

The tiny light from the smoke detector above the door-frame pierced the darkness, spearing straight to Janie Callahan's throbbing eyes. Crying for the last half-hour or so had proved useless; he wasn't going to hear her all the way in her office slash guest room, a whole entryway and door studded hallway from their bedroom. The light broke into two separate ones, pulling apart slowly like churning taffy in a machine under the influence of her used up eyelids, swollen and cupping hot tears until she closed them hard. Even though they hadn't had a fight, Janie certainly felt like it. Peter had left the room without a single word.

Janie considered the conversation she'd had with her mom earlier that afternoon. Her mother's gentle urging to leave Peter had mad her angry, made her want to rebel and stay with Peter if only to prove that she could! That she could keep things afloat! By herself! But, Janie knew that her mother wasn't trying to push her. She knew that her mom spoke out of genuine worry. Peter could be so wonderful and charming, though, and she wished he mom could see that! That her mom could see how he was with the children, playing on the floor with them... building towers with blocks and laughing as they knocked them down...

Yet, she couldn't even keep her husband in the same bed with her. With those words swimming around in her mind, Janie coated herself in thick exasperation. She was a failure as a human being. Why am I so restless lately, she begged her id for a concrete answer, why can't I help it? Janie knew that it was her own fault for keeping him awake, that Peter had work at the hospital early the next morning, but that made her feel all the worse for crying. Her pillow was wet. She waited in the cold bed, the room transformed by the dark into emptiness, her pillow flattened out. She felt very small looking at the emptiness stretched out over the white sheets and wondered if it would help any to get in the middle of the queen mattress instead of hovering on her own side, the left. No, because then if Peter came back and she had accidentally fallen asleep, which was highly unlikely, he may not want to bother to move her over, and then he would leave again.

Shooting a few cursory sobs into the night, she knew that he could not hear her. He wasn't coming back before morning. Maybe, she thought, I should go sleep on the couch. If he's not in our bed, I don't want to be either. Oh, but then the kitten would whine and Peter would think that I was pressing him for attention and come in to the living room upset, and that would make it worse. Giving up, she let her tears run free out of the prison her constricted muscles created, keeping them from escaping until now. She cried because the tears were there, and wouldn't stop being there, but did not cry with her voice.

Guilt washed off some splotches of her exasperation and made it even harder to bear. Her selfish wish for comfort from Peter for the fact that she couldn't sleep was disparaging. She felt guilt creep up again, in a slowly cresting wave, the fact eating away at her that she hated his job. Yes, at this moment, she hated it, though she would never tell him that. She was proud of him, he really was a brilliant OB/GYN surgeon, and wanted him to feel, in that manly necessary way, that she truly was proud, genuinely proud of the work that he did, slaving away at twelve-hour shifts just for her.

Usually, without more than a hint of a problem, she could dam it up inside her sensitive, prickly mind, but tonight during dinner, while Peter was recounting the day's events, he had said "got to" instead of "had to." And, he had smiled when he said it, but Janie wasn't sure if the smile was there from remembrance or spurred from the now. That had done it; the long-suppressed floodgates had opened and now all Janie could see were her husband's perfect hands in the act of medical examination. This was why, after all, people played doctor in bed, she thought, still trying to paint the ever-mounting images either all black or all white to conceal them completely from her mind's eye. The more she tried to kill them, the stronger they resurrected.

Peter's manicured fingers running along the skin of naked damsels in distress, searching for maladies. Is that what he did when he touched her, just out of practice? Look for maladies, mistakes, flaws? At least she had his lips to herself. Those were hers. As was his intimacy. But, his hands had been places and his eyes had been places that she wished that she could erase. At least he wore gloves. They did, didn't they? Wear gloves for everything like that? Janie didn't think she could ask him without shaking his faith that she had faith in him, which always results in less faith in the end.

He had promised that it would never happen again. After the second and third times, he promised. Except for when... Janie felt her shoulders shake.

Gloves made it a little better. No touch. Then she remembered the tee shirt. Peter had this shirt from school that said something like, "You know you're in medical school when a

116

classmate asks you to take it all off for research and you quickly obey."

He had been the only man Janie had ever been with, ever seen in the flesh, but she felt haunted by the dozens of others that had stood there in front of him, exposing themselves long before she had, indulging his curiosity in a wide variety of ways before she had gotten a chance to satisfy her own curiosity in only one direction. The one and only direction that she flung her entire heart and soul into, gave all of her love to. Why couldn't he work innocently in pediatrics or in podiatry or in allergies? He was such a handsome person, but the beauty didn't sink into his soul, she sadly admitted to herself.

chapter 11

EDMUND THUMBED THROUGH the phone book calling local hospitals. The only reason that Simon would have been in that kind of hurry is if something had happened to George. The look on Simon's face was that of horror. Something must have happened to George. He had to be in the hospital or something.

"Ah, yes, hello, is there a Mr., I mean, Dr. George Morris there?" Edmund repeated this sentence for the tenth time.

"No, sir, there isn't."

"Ma'am, is there not one because you're not allowed to tell me if there is, or is there really not anyone by that name there?"

"No, sir, there is no one by that name here. Sorry."

Before Edmund even heard the digital clicking sound of his cordless phone, his finger was already following the hospital listings, going down in alphabetical order. New York Presbyterian Hospital. He considered stopping the search, merely going to all of this trouble on a hunch, but dialed the number anyway.

***

"Maddy, I feel like I need to be up there! What if there's a change?"

"Agnes will call you. You need to be somewhere besides that hospital room for a few hours at least."

"Did she call while I was asleep?"

"Don't you think I would've let you know, Simon?"

"Well, yeah…"

"okay. Now, I'm getting back to work and you are going back to that couch."

"Yes, ma'am. I like it when you're bossy," Simon winked, weakly.

Maddy rolled her eyes and smiled at him, "March!"

"Yes, ah, Madeline Bryson of *The Times* here, looking for information on the burglary and assault of Dr. George Morris, Waterford Corporation?"

"One moment please." The voice on the phone was short.

"Simon! We're on hold again! Again! Oh, wait, here's somebody."

"Police Deputy Garrison speaking."

"Yes, sir, this is Madeline Bryson of *The Times*, and I was hoping that you would give us some information regarding the Dr. George Morris assault and burglary case."

"Well, ma'am… I'm not quite sure what you want, but…"

"Dr. Morris is an important man, Deputy Garrison. Our readers want to know what happened to him. Who the suspects are."

"Sorry, but we're not giving out that information at this time."

Maddy wasn't known to quit this easily. "Respectfully, sir, what time will you be giving out the information so I can be sure and call back?"

Maddy heard a quiet stroke of laughter on the line.

"A determined little lady, aren't ya?"

"Sir, I would really appreciate getting to the bottom of this. Why was Dr. Morris attacked?"

"Well, Miss…ah…"

"Bryson."

"Well, Miss Bryson, the most we can tell is that it was just a burglary gone bad."

"What was taken from the home?"

"Nothing that we can see."

"Electronics, nothing?"

"Nope."

"Why was Dr. Morris assaulted, then, sir?"

"Our leads are confidential at this time, little lady."

"I'd appreciate it, sir, if you'd speak to me in a more respectful tone…"

Maddy spoke the rest of her sentence into a silent receiver, "…in the future." The officer had hung up.

"Well, Simon, at least we tried." Maddy looked at Simon, his downcast face looking as if it were carefully examining the floor tiles. "I'll try again later, ask to speak to someone else," she added.

He looked up, "Really? Thanks."

When Maddy could tell that there was nothing more to do or say, she bid Simon adieu and walked back to work. It had been her lunch break and she had gone back to check on him, having taken him back to her place to crash on the couch and let him talk if he needed to. One the way, she replayed their conversation in her mind.

Maddy tended to need a little quality caffeine around noon, so she had picked them up some of the daily house brew at The Coffee Cup on the way to her apartment. She had been talking about the coffee being especially good and had interjected

something about enjoying talking with him and instead of reply-
ing in his own voice, Simon had given Maddy a quote as he did
periodically, like a present: "Good communication is as stimulating as black coffee and just as hard to sleep after."

Maddy had just loved that... loved the metaphor. Sponta-
neously, she flipped her phone open and hit the last dialed call.

"Hey, there!"

"Hey... Who was it who said your coffee quote?"

"Anne Morrow Lindbergh."

"Novelist?"

"Right."

"Thanks!"

"Sure..."

"That's all." Maddy started to say "bye" and hang up but
Simon persistence kept her from it.

"That's it? You just wanted to wake me up from the nap
you forced me to take, raid my trivia knowledge, and then make
me think about your voice for the rest of the day and not give me
anything to show for it?"

She laughed.

"All right then, Miss Bryson."

"Bye, then." Maddy said goodbye, but knew, or sort of
hoped, that more was coming. She loved Simon's teasing, despite
her equally teasing outward protests.

"Hey, how about a movie tonight?"

"Fine! It'll be good for you to get your mind off things."

"Okay."

"Perfect."

"Okay, then." They both paused. Laughed a little awkwardly. And, then both said goodbye at once. Even though
Simon seemed pleasant enough, Maddy could hear the looming

sadness in his voice. Something about it seemed flat, listless. Noticing its absence during their conversation, she had missed the childlike twinkle in his eye.

They had never once just gone to a movie on a date. Simon had made plans for picnics, boat rides, museum tours – but never a movie.

Maddy knew that even though they had not been dating long that she was willing to do whatever it took to get the joy back into him. It was her duty as a friend. She needed that buoyant joy now, needed it for the feeling it gave her and for the happiness that she knew that it gave others who knew him. Maddy would never dream of telling Simon to his face anything as sentimental and wishy-washy as what she had just confided to herself, afraid to appear too serious about their relationship in case he wasn't as serious as she was. Honestly, she wasn't sure how serious she was about it either. All she knew was that Simon was fun and easy to be around. She'd never actually enjoyed dating before and had never seen it as more than a pressured struggle to formulate interesting conversation between two nervous individuals out trying to impress one another.

***

As Simon slipped his cell into his pocket after talking with Maddy, it rang again and he immediately grabbed it out again.

"Hello?"

"Agnes!"

"George is fine. Relatively. Get some rest."

"Um... actually, I'm not calling about that. I've called because I had a thought!"

"What?"

"Emily!"

"Yes…"

"Has anyone checked George's accounts?"

"You're right! Simon, we've got to freeze them all! I'll get right on it."

"Thank you."

"Thank you for thinking of it. Maybe the police already have, but I'll check."

"No problem."

"George is lucky to have you as a friend, Simon."

"A pessimistic friend to even think of this, but a friend no less."

***

Pulling out from a bank ATM, about two hundred miles outside of the Mexican border, Emily pouted.

"They froze my checking account, baby!"

"No matter," Max answered, unusually calm.

"Do you think they know?"

"No, I'll bet it's just a legality. Since he's probably still in a coma."

"They can't do that! It's got my name on it, too!"

Emily made little puffs of dust as she stomped back to the car and they started off again. Max loved the anonymous feeling he had, cruising through the sea of asphalt. Cars with passengers of different races, different demographics racing around him than what was familiar back in New York. Texas was like another country! No one knew who he was and didn't care. The flight into Austin had been long, but unhampered. He was home free now and could get away with anything he wanted to.

The Times had even paid for his plane ticket, sending him off to Mexico City to cover some kind of changes to the trade agreement. He hadn't studied up on it because he wasn't planning to cover the story. This was his perfect opportunity to disappear with a large sum of cash.

It was a good plan with or without Emily's continued involvement, though he did intend to extract any information that Emily – a major stockholder in Chemi-Life – had on the new morality drug. He had been working on the story and saw Emily's name on the list. Blaine had a hunch that they knew something about what was going on. They'd have to. It was bringing in too much cash to the otherwise struggling Chemi-Life for them not to have looked into it a bit. Besides, his hunches were usually right, getting him where he was today. He had to trust it. It was his job to trust it. It was worth a little of his time if he could break the story from it. He wouldn't lose anything if the hunch was wrong, anyway.

After calling all the female stockholders and judging their voices, Blaine had decided to intimately befriend Emily and thus become the first reporter to get the whole story to the mass media. He might even get on national news if he could find out all the details of the scandal. This could do Chemi-Life in, and that was no small happening. They made everything! People used their stuff every day across the nation and if customers lost trust in them, thought they might die taking a couple of harmless Chemi-Life brand headache pills, the whole market could change. Besides that, no one had ever pulled such a big scam in the pharmaceutical industry and gotten past the FDA so easily. Maybe there were insiders in the Fed involved. That could make an even juicer story. He decided to play it all by ear.

Jessica D. Lovett

"We still have the stocks and the credit cards. Maybe we should cash them in, too, just in case somebody gets the wise idea to freeze those."

"Okay. Whatever." Emily, as was her general mood when not overly ecstatic, was indifferent.

At the red light at the access road, Max scoured the sights for another bank ATM machine. They stopped the car at one very old, rusty looking one and Emily sauntered out to it, swishing her hair-sprayed hair and dramatically lifting up her too-big-for-her-face sunglasses to read the LCD screen. She turned back to Max, visually enraged.

Emily jabbed her cards in and out, again and again, each one over and over until Max finally yelled out to her to give it up and get back in the car. She had the crinkled expression of a stressed toddler on the verge of a temper tantrum.

"Freezing's a legality. Besides, we have plenty of stocks and plenty of cash leftover. We have traveler's checks. We're fine without it. We've already milked enough out of your beloved husband to keep us set up for a while, especially where we're going."

Emily looked unconvinced.

"You're not just in it for the money, are you, doll?"

She shook her head no. Max grabbed her chin and pulled her face in his direction, kissing her implacably.

"Ow!" Emily rubbed her lips with the back of her hand.

"Sorry," Max quickly said. Emily admitted to herself that she was terrible with money and hadn't really kept up with the amount they had left after withdrawing several thousand before. She added it up in her head. Wasn't there more than that?

Max. He was probably hoarding some cash somewhere. Oh, well. He did make up for it. Max was exceptional. Much

126

better than anyone else she had been with, even if he could get a little too rough. At least that meant he was truly excited because of her. No comparison with George.

"Besides, we can always hock that gigantic rock of yours," Max laughed and grabbed up Emily's left hand, eying it for potential value, "since you're not in need of it anymore…"

"Right." She took her hand away.

"That sounded pretty unconvincing, Mrs. Morris." Max's eyebrows were raised.

"Of course I don't want to be married to boring George anymore! I hated every second! What do you think I'm doing now, running away? I want passion! I want to marry you, Max!"

"Right."

"Well, you said that…"

"Right, Emily, I know what I said."

***

Edmund walked into George's hospital room, one over-shined tile at a time. The nurses had asked him if he were with Agnes Bloom when he asked where George's room was. Judging by that, she must be a good friend. There was no slide-out food tray, no table space, so Edmund placed the daisies he had brought for George on the windowpane.

A red-haired nurse in scrubs with dogs and cats in the rain, wearing rainbow colored goulashes and slickers, stuck her head in the door, "You're George's friend? Maybe you can do a better job of springing him awake than we are. It'd do him good to snap out of this sleep."

All of a sudden, the nurse gasped and raced into the room in attack mode, with her eyes affixed on the flowers as if they were a dangerous masked intruder or something. She grabbed them up with such force that some white petals drifted to the floor. Without giving him a chance to defend himself, she started out of the room with them.

"Sorry, sir, but this is ICU. No flowers. I'll just place these on the nurse's station desk outside until your..." she looked at her watch, "twelve more minutes are up. Thank you for your cooperation."

"You're welcome, ma'am," Edmund said to the silent room.

***

Simon waved to the nurses whose faces had become familiar to him on the way to the waiting room to meet Agnes. She was quietly knitting something – he couldn't tell what yet – in the corner.

"Hey, I'm here."

"Hello, Simon. Glad you got some rest."

"Well, it's your turn now, Agnes, you've been up here nonstop."

"Maybe in a little while. Let's go see him again, together?

As they walked down the hall, Agnes took his arm. He had never before noticed the frailty in her. Then again, maybe it hadn't been there before this. Approaching the room, the nurse behind the desk told them that someone was in there with George right now and they would have to wait their turn. Agnes and Simon both looked at each other, shocked.

"Emily?!" they both whispered.

"You go, Simon, there's no telling what I'd say to the woman."

Agnes hunkered down in a chair a few yards away, rummaged in her big purse, and began aggressively knitting, eyes focused on Simon and not on her work. Simon shrugged at her, indicating that he didn't know what to say either, but Agnes's hand gestures pushed Simon in the door. He felt relief wash over him.

"Oh, um, hello! I'm Simon. Do you know George from work?"

When Edmund turned around from beside the window, where he had been picking up the few petals that had fallen from his contraband daisies, Simon saw his face. It took him a minute to place Edmund, that brief moment it takes for one's brain to register a somewhat familiar face when it is put in an unfamiliar setting.

"Hello, Simon."

"Edmund. Well, I... ah... I didn't know that you and George were close really..."

"Simon, I've been wanting to tell you both something. About who I am. I'm... Well, I'm not really a doorman."

"Oh, you've been doing a fine job," Simon interrupted, "Everyone doesn't feel 'real' when they're first in a job. What did you do before? The economic times hitting you?"

"Simon, listen to me." Edmund let loose a small fake-sounding laugh, "This is sort of embarrassing to say. I don't know how to..."

"Just say it!" Simon's curiosity showed in his voice.

"Well, Simon... I'm... I'm..."

"What?"

"I'm George's father-in-law."

"What?!?" Simon repeated himself, with much more emotion than he intended to leak out.

***

Maddy floated into work and wove through the desks to her area. Distracted by so much, her gaze landed on Kirby Holmes's monitor, when she usually tried to give her coworkers the respect of not peeking in on the stories they were working on. "Chemi-Life Morality Drug Scandal" was in bold print across the top of the document as Kirby typed furiously. Maddy's eyes scanned the text, picking out the words "religion pill," "multiple deaths," "neglect of the FDA," "lying advertisements," and "fudged test results." She stopped walking. Then she saw the list of major stockholders who could possibly be involved. Emily Morris was on the list. It had to be a different Emily Morris! The last sentence Kirby had written read, "None of the major stockholders could be reached for comment."

She couldn't help herself. She would have to be nice to Kirby and hope he forgave her for rejecting him over and over enough to share some information.

"So, ah, Kirby. What's this you're working on? What's this Chemi-Life thing?"

"Hello, Bryson. Just one of the biggest stories ever! Well, biggest for me."

"What's going on?"

"Chemi-Life, this huge company, could be put under for this! They released a drug too early and made sure the test results looked positive to the FDA, thinking that they were on to something big that the public would buy in a heartbeat. Funny thing is, it made hearts stop beating!" Kirby erupted in goofy laughter.

"Kirby! That is not funny! People have died? Those are people's family members, best friends!"

"Yeah, yeah, Bryson, you're right. Sorry," Kirby sniffed slightly and stifled his giggles. "Some kind of thick-skinned, weathered reporter you are, Bryson!"

"Why did you call it the 'religion pill'?" Maddy asked, ignoring Kirby's comment.

"It messed with people's brains and made them more focused and awake and stuff like a regular cognitive enhancer, but it also made people act nice."

"You mean calm. An anti-depressant."

"No, nice. It made people kinder, more social, want to be a better person."

"How is that possible?"

"I don't know. I'm researching it right now. Moral steroids. Also known as 'Ghandhi' pills."

"You've tried calling the stockholders?"

"Yep. None will give me anything."

"Can I see your list of numbers?"

"Why?"

"I have personal interest in this."

After a long tirade with Maddy finally agreeing to go out for coffee with Kirby sometime, he finally handed it over. Kirby was so pushy that she thought maybe she would bring Simon along as protection if she had to actually go for coffee with him. She didn't say she wouldn't bring her boyfriend after all, if Simon were indeed her boyfriend. Maddy dialed the number listed for Emily Morris on the phone in her cubicle. She had no idea what she would say if someone answered. Maybe it was Emily's cell and she could question her about George, if it were the same Emily Morris. There could feasibly be more than one in New York. It's not an altogether uncommon name, Maddy told herself.

After a few rings, an answering machine picked up. George's voice came on the line, the voice that had now been silenced for who knows how many hours now. "You've reached the Morris residence - Emily, George, and Darby. Please leave us a message. Thanks!" Cheerful enough. No one would suspect that they were so unhappy a household. But why was Emily a major stockholder at Chemi-Life? How could she have the brains to do that? Maybe George had default stock, as an employee. Yet, that still wouldn't make him a major stockholder. And, they were having money problems, weren't they? Simon had confided that in her. She had talked with herself George and could see the worry in his face. Major stockholders don't generally worry about paying bills on time, do they? Maddy took the list back to Kirby's desk.

"You find what you were looking for, Bryson?"

"Sort of. Thanks."

chapter 12

SIMON HAD MOTIONED for Agnes to come over and she had reluctantly obeyed. The nurse at the desk had, at first, started to complain about the one-person-at-a-time rule, but Agnes dutifully stood in the open doorway of the room next to Simon.

"I don't understand. George never told me that the doorman was his father-in-law. He told me that you looked familiar, like somebody, though. That would explain that. You must look like his wife!"

Simon was livid. There was too much happening at the same time. His ears felt hot as he looked upon his IV-stabbed friend across the room, a striped and beaded-with-age hospital gown messily falling down George's shoulder. Ignoring the rule, Simon went into the room, reached down and straightened it, tying the knot at the neckline and pulling down the rest under the white hospital sheets. He straightened those, too, out of nervousness.

He jumped when he saw a speck of blood on the cotton, his sudden move accidentally causing some tube or other get a little twisted. To Simon's dismay, it started to beep at him. A nurse came running to adjust some of the mysterious dials and push buttons to appease the beeping monstrous contraption. She glanced at Simon pointedly for being the second visitor in the room, and also for setting off the machine, but Edmund duti-fully went into the hallway.

"He didn't know me, Simon. We hadn't ever met."

"Wait! You're lying, Edmund!" Simon raised his voice confidently.

"What do you mean?"

"I seem to remember George telling me that Emily's parents had died. Before college. Just like his did, in a car accident. That was a kind of bond that they had. One of the only ones."

"Another lie from Emily, not from myself."

"Okay. I'd believe that."

"Me, too," Agnes chimed in.

***

Emily stared out the window, not really looking at anything. Max took his right hand off the steering wheel and began to play with the hem of her denim miniskirt.

"You never did tell me the whole story about how you got those stocks, Emily."

"Thought I did tell ya."

"No, you told me that you bribed somebody and that you were now a major holder, but you didn't spill the details. I just don't see how you did it. I didn't know you knew anything about the stock market."

"Nothing to know, really. I went down to George's old office with the divorce papers, kinda mad and everything, and I forgot that he had told me he'd changed offices. There wasn't a secretary there so I went past and threw open the doors, ready to show George the papers, but these bigwigs were having a meeting. They didn't believe me that I didn't hear anything and thought I must have listened for a bit. I did hear a little, about some pill and people dying from it and stuff."

"And?"

"And, they offered me stock to keep my mouth shut and I said no, that I wanted more and more or I'd tell it all, that I had friends in the press, so they gave it to me."

"But you really don't know anything about the pill?"

"Nope. Not really."

"Do you have friends in the press?"

"No, but George has a friend who is sort of a writer."

"You, Emily, are such a liar," Max said, hitting the wheel with the heel of his palm.

"How do you know I'm not lying to you, then, Max?" Emily added, trying to change the subject.

"I can tell that you're not. I know you need me, Mrs. Morris. You wouldn't have left everything if you didn't."

"Maybe I was just bored!" Emily shot back at him, her eyes angry slits.

"Maybe, but I think you need me." Max stretched one arm and then the other, keeping control of the steering wheel as he did.

"Hey, did you see me pack those divorce papers, Max? I'm sure I did, but I can't find them," Emily reached her arms to fumble with her suitcase in the backseat, hanging halfway between the front passenger and back seats of the car.

"Haven't seen them, but you do need me Mrs. Morris. You just don't know if I need you or not and I intend to keep it that way."

When Max wouldn't return her trying-to-be-piercing glances, Emily leaned her chair all the way back and pretended to take a nap.

Jessica D. Lovett

***

Maddy still had questions. Maybe Kirby could answer them. It was worth a try.

"So, Kirby... no offense, but why are *you* doing this story? Aren't you usually assigned to more, you know..."

Kirby stopped her before she could finish and possibly hurt his ego.

"Maxwell was working on it, he had a contact that he was getting direct info out of, but he had to go out of town so they gave it to me. I guess I'm on probation. Kind of like you, Bryson," Kirby smiled a sideways smile. "He's going to be miffed when he sees my name above that article. I'll be sure and site him in there... say thanks..."

"How did you know about that?"

"I'm nosey. I'm a reporter. That's my job."

"Fine. Where's Blaine?"

"Mexico City."

"Why in the world is he there?"

"Covering the new changes to NAFTA. Minor changes, but still a big deal to a lot of people."

They talked for a few minutes more about less important things, Maddy on conversation auto-pilot after she had gotten all that she could out of Kirby. This all seemed strange to her. Why didn't Blaine tell her he was leaving? That alone was strange. Maybe he had seen her with Simon and had given up on trying to go out with her. All for the better, since, Maddy rationalized, she really liked Simon and Blaine was just a handsome-yet-hollow temptation to get in the way.

Maddy felt her cell vibrate and saw Simon's name in the window.

136

"Hello?" Even though Maddy knew who it was via the caller ID, she never felt comfortable just answering someone, like she knew who it was already, as if that took away some sort of privacy they had.

"Hey, Maddy, can I see you tonight?"

Simon never failed to mince words, did he?

"Sure. What... ah... where do you..."

"My place?" Simon cooed.

"Well, I ah..."

"I'm an honorable gentleman, I promise. I have something to give you there."

"That doesn't sound too honorable!" Maddy joked.

"I'm serious! I have a actual, wrapped, in-a-box present for you there."

"Well, okay, Simon. See you later."

***

"That's absolutely terrible!" Agnes held her hands to her cheeks. Simon leaned against the windowsill and shook his head. "Wow" was all he could say. He had just stepped out for one second to call Maddy when it seemed like they were just casually talking and he already felt like he had missed the big parts of this story.

"Why now, though, Edmund? Why try and make up with Emily now?"

"No particular concrete reason other than that I just got tired of living with myself. I didn't want to be someone with no family because of choice, estranged from my daughter because of my inaction."

"That's such a painful thing to live with," Agnes sighed, "but don't be so hard on yourself! My only daughter, Janie, is giving me a tough time, too. On a different level than this, though. Her husband, Peter, is a cheating, abusive cad. I wish that... well, no, I'm not going to say that. I just wish that I could somehow protect her from the pain of all this."

"Just as I wished that I could protect Emily from the pain, even though it was my fault in the first place. She would never let me protect her, not even as a curious toddler. She'd leap in to everything, head first and headstrong."

"That's my Janie, too, Edmund. We just can't protect them, can we? We just have to pray."

"In other words, pretend you're doing something about it by comforting yourself, convincing yourself that you're taking action by speaking to some higher power," Edmund philosophized.

"No, I mean kneeling at the throne of the most powerful force for good in the universe and pleading for forgiveness and mercy into the lives of those he created and already loves more than we could ever imagine," Agnes countered.

"Halt! No. I am not getting into this conversation right now. We're all under pressure here," Simon tried to help.

"You'd do good to get into it, Simon. Sometimes a man's got to be brave and stand up for something, not be the neutral. That's what my late husband, James, would always say. Don't be the neutral."

There was a knock at the door and two nurses came in with a new IV and some bandages to clean George's wounds. Agnes, Simon, and Edmund closed the door and left their perch in the doorway to let the nurses do their job, giving George a little dignity.

***

Janie had been taken in, just like all the other girls were, with Peter's strong, chiseled features, his perfect... his perfect everything. Janie had forgotten to strip that all away and see his emotionally-arthritic heart before saying yes when he romantically swooped down on one knee with that huge diamond and all those huge dreams... He could make anything sound wonderful. In a twisted way, she didn't blame those women – the three that she knew about, at least – for being taken in by him. He was a very overwhelming person. One who demanded to be obeyed... and forgiven.

Peter saying that they were only patients and didn't mean anything to him only made it worse. "It doesn't mean anything" was what people said after an affair when trying to make up with the betrayed spouse. They had had such a nice evening together, a nice dinner, nice conversation – why was she trying to mess it up? Hours ago, when Peter was still on the right side of the bed, Janie had decided that it was better to ease her mind now and be honest than to suffer all night alone. She had cautiously whispered into the night, "Are you awake?" She was sort of wishing that he would be asleep. He didn't reply. The silence disappointed her anyway.

Living one's life in the purely physically and being trained to ignore the spiritual elements had consequences, it would seem to Janie. Did Peter really feel the intense impact that his physical grievances had on Janie, the corroding of her spirit its fallout caused, so long after the initial blow? The second time it happened had been a surprise attack. People could possibly make the same mistake twice, Janie had reasoned. But, then the last one... The last one had taken her out.

Maybe the dividing line between the physical and all else for Peter was so bold, so strong and tall and vast, that he couldn't even see past it if he wanted to. He was expertly trained to solve physical problems, not emotional ones. Janie had to give him that. He was definitely an expert. Yet, it had been, what, a year? She'd forced herself to stop counting the "safe" days since his trespass long ago.

They had already had this conversation. She concentrated on reliving it in her mind, hopefully to stop the tears that were already forming. Janie decided that it was just beyond his professional understanding, as was her aversion to blood and guts in movies or in real life almost equally. He thought that she should be strong and get past it. To her, every pain-brimming image replaced at least three elevated memories. It was simply a case of saving good memories from being unworthily sacrificed. He had apologized. It was over. The physical sins had been eradicated, at least in his eyes.

Peter would also rationalize that it must mean that she did not trust him fully or think that he was good at what he did. What did trust and competence have to do with absorbing sensations and memories of naked women that were not one's wife, under any circumstances? Especially with one prone to unfaithfulness...

Sometimes things would remind her. Janie always knew where he was, but never what he was doing. At any moment he could be touching another woman's likely larger breasts, or worse. When Peter had said that he "loved" his job, the unpredictability, the variety of it, she'd taken it the wrong way, enough for him to notice that she had. In an attempt to ease her mind, he'd said that some things are better without variety. All that this accomplished was making her feel as if she was some kind of boring, tedious routine.

This last set of thoughts had ushered her into a lull. Not real sleep exactly, but a state of non-thought or perhaps a prolonged single thought that turned into a wall to block out all of the others banging against each other. Just as the heavy curtain had lowered itself, and the stream of tears had run dry, the door opened, letting light pour into the room in a triangular shape, jutting out confidently from the doorframe.

Peter bent down to her side of the bed and said through a hearty hug, "I hope that I didn't keep you awake last night, honey. I finally went into your office so I wouldn't. I just knew that I was keeping you up." "No, that's all right. Thanks," Janie managed to say. Tears began to gather, joining forces behind her eyes to fight her resolve. "I was dwelling too much on work again. Got to go in a few minutes." He loved her. She hated being the untrusting wife speculating about speculums. Upon further examination, Janie decided that the best thing to do was keep quiet.

***

With nothing else to say and no reason to stay at the hospital, Edmund trudged back to his apartment. He had quit the job as the building's doorman and would be going back to Texas soon. Edmund had finally sold the house in Jefferson, hopefully selling off some of the memories attached to it and had decided to go on with his life. No good had come from holding on to his old life all these many years, preserving it just in case Emily decided to come back. Just in case his wife or his son magically reappeared in a long-forgotten memory triggered by that place. He knew he'd go home to Texas, having been born and raised a Texan, but he had yet to decide where to make his new start.

chapter 13

SIMON ANXIOUSLY ANSWERED his cell, seeing it was George's office phone number. Agnes had said that she needed to go back to work but they had assured each other that they would call the other if there were any changes to George's condition between their individual hospital visits.

"Simon! Guess what!"

"What, what, what?"

"George is speaking! Whispering softly, with much effort, but still speaking! He's out of it, Simon, he's out of it!"

"That's awesome! I'll be there in one second."

"Great. This has been the longest two days in my life."

"Me, too. Hey, Agnes?"

"Yes?"

"What did he say?"

"Oh, he just said my name."

"Well, that means he remembers something!"

"Let's just hope he doesn't go back into the coma. And, let's just hope – and pray! – that George is his old self again and that we haven't lost him."

"I'll try my best. I'm good at hoping."

***

"Hold on, Max, I need to take this call. It's my daughter."

Max let his thoughts wander as he halfway listened to Emily's conversation with Marlena, her thirteen-year-old daughter that Emily had stashed in a ritzy boarding school in London since she was tiny. Emily was a kinder person on the phone with Marlena. Not motherly, exactly, just nicer. Max wished that she would let her guard down and be wholeheartedly kind to him for once. He guessed it was partly his fault, his abrasive personality. People never seemed to be completely themselves with him. Yet, it would make what he had to do next harder if she had been kinder to him.

Though he was too much in the physical moment to feel sorry for George as they were fighting, Max was human enough to feel a twinge of pity for him now. Emily certainly had put George through the wringer. She had lied about everything and he – being a trusting sort – had believed her unquestioningly. Max questioned everything, tended to think that everyone, no matter what, had some sort of angle. George just wasn't that way. He had some kind of screw loose in his brain in the logical thinking section, Max surmised. Hadn't he suspected any of this? Could anyone really be that naïve?

Emily had told Max all about Marlena about a month into their relationship, though he did not know why she felt at ease enough to confide about it. She had told him that she had never let anyone else know about Marlena, not even George. She had said that George thought that the frequent phone calls from Marlena were from Emily's fabricated sister, Cindy Jarvis. That George had always wanted kids and would have probably been amicable enough about adopting Marlena, but if Emily told him about the girl, it would tell him everything... that Emily had lied about her age when they were in college, that she had lied about her name, that she had lied about her virginity being given to him on their wedding night – all of it. Max had watched as the whole pretty picture of an ideal marriage that Emily created for herself had started to crash down around her ankles. Or, perhaps it had started breaking up before Max had even met Emily.

It was a pretty rich story... Max didn't remember all the details – Emily could prattle on so – but he did remember how that Emily had been so depressed after college about her mother and her brother, Eddie Joe, that she had transformed herself away from it all. She'd gone from being a quiet homebody, like she described father as, to something of a party animal. Emily had wanted no similarities left between her father and herself. As a result, she had had an affair with a NFL football player from Dallas, resulting in a baby girl. When Marlena was born, the football player had promised to pay for everything for the baby. He still sent the checks to the expensive boarding school that Emily had chosen for Marlena.

"Tell you about your father? Well, Eddie Joe was a sweet man. He loved music and going to the movies. Why, we'd go every weekend we could..." Emily prattled on to Marlena.

When she had hung up, Max questioned her. There was so much that was a lie in her life, he didn't know how she kept it all straight.

"Wait a sec... I thought that Eddie Joe was your brother."

"He was."

"Eddie Joe was the incestuous father of your baby and also a pro football player?"

"No, of course not, silly. Calvin's her daddy. I told Marlena that Eddie Joe was her daddy once because I knew all the little details about him and it was easier to sound like we'd been married. That she had been born, you know, when her mama and daddy were married and all. She knows that Eddie Joe died in a hunting accident. That explains everything away. Why her daddy is not in her life."

"That's cruel."

"What's more cruel? That, or knowing that you were an accident, that your mama slept around with a football team and that your daddy is a famous hulk who never calls or cares or does anything for you except pay the bills?"

Max didn't answer.

"Besides, I took on my mama's maiden name, Jarvis, when I decided to go back to college again and cut off anything connected to my father. Start a new life away from him. College was the happiest time in my life and I knew I could find happiness going there again. Pretend to be seven years younger. With my looks, I did it easy! It was just as easy to get fake birth certificates and all that. Real easy. I could've been a spy!" Emily laughed.

Max still didn't say anything, acting like that he was deeply concentrating on driving the car down the sparse highway.

"Anyway, Eddie Joe Hopkins. So, I could casually show Marlena documents saying my name had been Emily Hopkins. She'd believe me. Not think that her mama was a liar."

"But her mother is a liar."

"She'll never know. And, I did find happiness going back to school again. I got another liberal arts degree – with A's instead of C's the next time around – got engaged to George Morris, an aspiring chemical engineer, and we had a fairy tale wedding. I still got a white dress even though I'd had a baby. Proper Southern women can't wear white dresses at their wedding if people know that they've been with someone, you know."

"Are you happy now?"

"I've got you, Max!"

"Do you?"

With this her eyes narrowed down to little almost-invisible slits, making wrinkles around her eyes that she usually consciously avoided creating by choosing mostly neutral, indifferent, yet still beautiful expressions.

"Yes, I think I do. I'm good enough for you, aren't I?"

"Pretty good, Mrs. Morris."

"I wish you'd stop calling me that, Max. I really hate it."

***

Maddy tossed her crossed leg up and down, keeping time with Simon's music the back of her heel on his couch. She looked down and skimmed the carpet with her eyes. Simon noted her nervousness. Should he put his arm around her now? Would it make her feel more or less nervous? More, probably.

"So, what's my surprise?" Maddy slowed her momentum until she'd stopped tossing her foot.

"Well, Maddy... you know that I think that it's very important to have a close, intimate friend. Someone to share your life with and to get to know your little habits, you know, like..." Simon paused, "oh, I don't know..."

He peered over and gauged Maddy's reaction to this. Worried? Check. Eyebrows raised? Check. He tried not to laugh. He had to fake a cough to hide a laugh that snuck out before he could catch it.

"It's so very important to have someone to hold as you drift off to sleep, a familiar face to stare into when you wake up in the morning, as you come out of your dreams..." Maddy started tossing her foot again. Simon kept going. Maddy seemed to have stopped breathing.

"But this kind of commitment, this kind of deep relationship cannot be taken lightly. I want your real, honest opinion on whether you want to try, just try, living with... with..."

Maddy had stopped breathing altogether. Maybe her heart had stopped, too, he couldn't tell. She crossed her arms against her chest.

"Gertrude the Guinea Pig, here!"

Simon reached behind the overstuffed chair in the corner, cleared off the prop of laundry hiding his surprise, and took out a pet carrier. Inside was a tiny, baby guinea pig with black and white spots and fur sticking up in every direction.

"She's an Abyssinian," Simon explained gingerly, stroking Gertrude until she started purring, "that's why her hair is all crazy like that."

"Simon, you cad! You scared me to death!"

Simon checked her expression to see if it was alright to laugh or if he should look repentant. Yet, he couldn't help it. He had to laugh a little. Maddy had turned totally white all over but still managed to blush in perfect red circles on her cheeks, like a porcelain doll. He thought it was beautiful. He'd have to think of ways to make her blush like this more often.

***

George sighed into the side of his pillow. Was it really morning again? How many mornings had he been like this? He'd stopped trying to label the days with names that didn't matter to him anymore. They just didn't stick.

148

For some unforeseen reason, the hospital had seen fit to send him home. Could it be that they were just tired of taking care of him? Or, needed his room for someone else? Though George admitted that he actually could move his arms slightly up and down with considerable effort, he felt just the same as he did on the first day that he could actually remember remembering. Plain terrible.

Sometimes he'd forget his injuries and try to jump up and go get a drink out of the fridge or grab a book off the shelf, like a person who forgets for a moment that their bedroom light bulb is out and tries to flip the switch. He'd have the impulse and start mentally to move off the couch, but then, no other parts of him would follow his lead.

George scanned the room. Usually kept in pristine condition by a cleaning crew that they'd hired at Emily's request, things were in a foreign disarray. The couch was crooked. The silk flowers had been turned over upside down and then turned right side up again, but not rearranged, so that the leaves and petals skewed out, mashed and mangled, in all directions, as if they were holding up an invisible beach ball.

He had almost forgotten that Simon and Agnes were there, compulsively keeping him company as if they were paranoid that he might keel over at any moment if their staring at him stopped. Simon materialized his presence in George's mind by piping up with a too cheery, "You okay?" George did not, could not, answer. He was okay in the since that he was alive, but not in any other sense. Without addressing Simon's question, George asked him one.

"What is that?"

"What?" Simon looked in the direction that George was looking.

149

Jessica D. Lovett

"Those papers over there, sticking out of the box under the table."

George tried to point, but his fingers and arm wouldn't cooperate. He gestured with his eyes toward the table – the table where the police had found his bleeding, unconscious body after neighbors had complained of loud shouting and banging coming from his home. He had found that part out later. George's nearest neighbors were an acre off. That must have been some loud commotion.

Simon caught his gesture and wound his way around misplaced furniture and little pieces of broken glass that had alluded Agnes's dustpan to the papers in question. They were in a small box sticking out from behind the half moon shaped table, no longer against the wall and underneath its matching mirror.

"The police gave me that box of stuff later. I was over here cleaning up a little and they called and dropped it by. I haven't really dug through it. I didn't feel it was my place," Agnes noted.

Simon picked them up but did not speak.

"Speak, man, speak!" George clamored. The papers must have been witnesses of the fight. Through the bloodstains that had evidently trailed across the ceramic tile onto the thick mass of pages, like a glaring red marker editing the typed text. Simon's eyes traced silently on and on.

"What?" George demanded again. Agnes, who had been unusually silent until a few moments ago, added her two cents in as well.

"I don't want to say."

"Hand it over," Agnes sighed.

When George almost could not stand it anymore, Agnes said it, those dripping, miserable words that he'd been dreaded all along.

"Divorce papers."

***

Maddy wiped stray tears off of her phone and onto her Indiana University sweatshirt. It was her day off. She had called to check on Jed Engle. Though she had only come to visit a handful of times, Maddy felt very close to the old man.

"Oh. I see. When exactly did it happen?"

Maddy had only asked if Jed was still in his room, meaning had he left for the mid-morning dominos game in the entertainment lobby yet, when the nurse had replied that, no, the funeral home had already taken him.

"Early this morning, actually. How did you know he had passed?"

"I didn't. Jed just was... was good at cheering me up and I thought I'd come and visit, so I thought I'd call and check and see if it was a 'good day' for him first."

Silence.

"After that interview, he was sort of a surrogate grandfather to me, I guess. My family is all..."

Maddy stopped herself. She needed to stop babbling aimlessly to this stranger. Well, not that it mattered. The stranger was actually listening. But, she was a nursing home nurse. That's what she did all day. Listen to emotional people, hear sadness and try to comfort it just by standing and opening her ears. Or, at least pretending to.

"Interview?" the faceless voice on the other line asked.

"Yes, he had a vivid life. I did a story on several veteran's stories for Veteran's Day last November."

Jessica D. Lovett

Maddy pictured the nurse in a white dress with hat and matching shoes, but she knew this wasn't so.

"What was wrong? Jed seemed so healthy."

"Well, the doctors feel it was a bad reaction to a new medicine that he had been started on for his depression. Besides just missing his family, Jed's battle fatigue had been flaring up again lately, giving him problems sleeping especially."

Maddy saw the headline that Kirby had been typing the day before. Maddy couldn't remember the scientific name of the drug, but she certainly remembered the manufacturer, George's company.

"Was it by any chance manufactured by Chemi-Life?"

"Actually, I believe so. How did you know?"

"Just a wild guess."

Now Maddy was mad. She was definitely going to get to the bottom of this.

"You should read next week's morning edition of *The Times*, ma'am. An article coming out by Kirby Holmes. Please tell your doctors to read it as well."

She threw her cellphone, diseased with the miserable news, on to the couch. The rest of the day Maddy kept hearing Jed's smiling voice saying, "Well, my story's about as dull as my pocket knife, little lady, but you print whatever you want."

***

Simon waited, on hold. Finally someone picked up. He was getting tired of this. Didn't these guys have any brains at all? What about all the movies he'd seen about the brave NYPD? Sending the divorce papers and all that stuff back to George's house in a box was ridiculous.

152

"NYPD. Detective Michaels speaking."

"Yes, this is Simon Kincade. I'm a friend of George Morris and I found some evidence about his assault case."

"Okay, just a sec."

Simon heard papers rummaging.

"Go ahead. Shoot."

"In the box of stuff returned from the police to his home, we found divorce papers. Bloodstained and unsigned by both parties. I, we, believe that this is obvious to the root of the crime and that Emily Morris, George's wife, needs to be found and that…"

Detective Michaels interrupted, not letting Simon go any further.

"Yes, Mr. Kincade. All of this has been noted. Ms. Morris has been located en route to the Mexican border. She is using a passport with her maiden name, Hopkins. We are currently watching her."

"Why'd you let her get away?" Simon was horrified.

"We didn't. We are observing the suspect. Currently there is not enough evidence to convict her. We are waiting to see if some crops up."

"Why weren't the divorce papers kept for evidence? Couldn't anyone see the importance of that? They have blood on them!"

"Yes, sir. They were found near the victim's body, underneath a table. There was enough blood at the scene that they got soiled. The papers have been properly scanned and taken record of. Of course they're important to the case."

"Why were they returned?"

"After careful debate, we decided that they best thing to do would be to return them and see if they got filed. We had no

153

way of knowing if the victim was aware of the documents or if the fight was about the signing of the documents."

"I know that he had no clue about them!" Simon nearly shouted.

"No offense, but some person just 'knowing' isn't enough. We need evidence. We decided to release the documents back into the house to see what would arise from that."

"What if she goes over the border? Can you still detain her after that?"

"Sir... we have not spoken to the victim yet. He is able to speak now, correct?"

"Yes he is, but isn't it obvious that she's running away from the crime?"

"Measures have already been taken, Mr. Kincade. That is all I can tell you. We are working closely with the police forces of that jurisdiction. Just leave it to us."

"Well, good. I'll try."

They hung up. Simon felt a little guilty about his earlier accusations. They did sound like they knew what they were doing. Hopefully they did. Simon still didn't feel too sure about this. He hated not taking action himself, he just had to find some action to take.

chapter 14

GEORGE RUBBED HIS eyes. Edmund pulled the blankets up a little higher around George. Grumpily trying to pull them down again, George grunted at the increased weight that everything around him suddenly had.

"How can I believe this? My wife has always told me you died! That, rather, her father died, whether you are her father or not. This is all very sketchy."

"Just look," Edmund flipped through his wallet. He pulled out a family photo taken when Emily was, judging from her looks, about eight. George stared. He had never seen the picture before, but it was obviously Emily and it was also easy to see Edmund's face in the much younger version of himself. George also saw that Edmund's hand rested on the shoulder of a little boy who looked a little younger than Emily.

Funny, he looked just like Emily would look as a boy, George thought. The male version of her exactly. Eddie Joe and Emily both had the same striking eyes and he could tell now that they got them from Edmund. George knew that something had bothered him about Edmund looking vaguely familiar when he first started the job at Simon's building. In just about every other physical way except her eyes, he guessed that Emily must favor her mother.

"Where's Cindy?"

"Who's Cindy, George?"

"Emily's younger sister. Lives in London. Your daughter!"

Edmund's eyebrows wove together as he considered who this Cindy person might possibly be.

"Sorry, George, must be another lie. The only children that Mary and I had were Emily first and then," Edmund hesitated, "Eddie Joe. Edmund, Jr."

"A brother! Why would she lie about that? That makes no sense!"

"Eddie Joe was killed. The month after his twentieth birthday. As can be expected, it was extremely difficult for Emily. They were always very close."

George just stared, so Edmund went on.

"Emily was twenty-five at the time. Her mother died two long years later. Our family had already fallen apart before Mary's passing though..."

"No car accident," George managed to say, mostly to himself.

"Right. No car accident."

"My parents died in a car accident the summer before my freshman year in college and she always said hers did, too. We had commonality in our suffering over those tragedies in our lives."

"And, about Cindy," Edmund bent over and rubbed the knuckles of one hand with the heel of his other one.

"Arthritis?" George interrupted casually.

"Yep. Mostly in there," he indicated to the white splotches on knuckles of both hands, rotating his self-massage.

"But, Edmund, I have the phone bills to London. She calls Cindy all the time. I met her at the wedding stuff – rehearsal dinner and all that! Cindy was the only family I met, so if she's not real, then..."

"I know how jarring this must be for you. I think I may have 'Cindy' figured out, now that you mentioned that she lives in London."

"What? Emily's cell phonebook says Cindy Jarvis!"

"Jarvis is Emily's mother's maiden name. Emily took it when she decided that she hated me for what I did... hated me for what happened."

"What?! What happened?"

"Let's go in order, George. This is getting to be too much for me, too."

"Fine." George leaned back, bracing himself for the long version of the story, but then all at once his eyes widened and his jaw became tight.

"What?" Edmund paused, patiently.

"Eddie Joe died after we got married? That can't be right! When we got married, Emily'd just finished school. She was twenty-two. I had finished a couple of years before, had been working, everything was great."

"Oh, George... this is too deep," Edmund stretched out flat on the richly patterned carpet, still absent-mindedly rubbing his hands together.

"What now?" George closed his eyes. "I'm ready. Give it all to me."

***

Emily and Max had stopped at a dingy motel. Max was sleeping, but his snoring kept Emily awake. They had never actually tried to sleep through the night together, she thought.

Jessica D. Lovett

The only person that Emily had ever done that with – truly slept all night – was George. Somehow, right now, it felt to Emily a more intimate thing than bumping pelvises was. Giving your asleep, vulnerable, unconscious self to someone was much more difficult.

She had no idea what the plan was now. They had escaped together and that had been as far as her mental planning had gone. Admittedly, she had never been good at thinking in the long term. Emily felt that one of her talents was making things up as she went along, keeping the details in line with the last story. It was a challenge, playing with life like that. In the back of her mind, Emily saw the faces of her mother and father. She had tried so desperately to create a new life for herself. Why couldn't she escape the old one?

The last time that Emily had seen her father was her peripheral view of him, his arm around the old, cracked porch column as she drove off in a pickup with some boy after deciding to go back to college again to get away. What was his name again? Oh, yeah – Kenneth. Kenneth Wilson. Someone of little consequence in her life, poor Kenneth Wilson will forever be stuck inside of one of the most terrible memories of Emily's life.

It was that moment that Emily had known that she would never have the luxury of going back home again for Thanksgiving or Christmas, smelling familiar scents, catching any gently falling memories of her childhood in her hands once more. Not anyone's sister or anyone's daughter any longer, Emily was completely and totally alone. The third most terrible memory.

The blame for her first most terrible memory would of course belong to her father, this being the very reason she drove away with Kenneth in the first place – running away just to get away from Edmund and the feelings he conjured. No matter how hard she had tried at first, Emily could never force herself to swallow down a belief that all that had happened had not been entirely her father's fault.

Emily had thought that she could escape the memory's iron grasp on her every waking thought by putting as many miles as possible between her and the place it all happened, but it had taken her years to live a day without seeing Edmund walking up the worn country trail holding her little brother, Eddie. His life-less body had been slung over Edmund's shoulders, arms holding arms. Blood streamed down both sides of Edmund's camouflage like two identical bold stripes on the front of his shirt. When they had gotten closer to her mother and herself, she could see that Edmund's tears had been streaming from his two eyes directly into the two red stripes.

Both Eddie's and Edmund's deer rifles were strapped to Edmund's back, the barrels sticking out from under Eddie's arms on either side. The coroner had insisted that it had been a fluke shot, happening to hit Eddie in precisely the right spot to kill him instantly. Soon thereafter, after the fights and the cold cloud of misery that accompany such an event as this, Emily's mother had died.

In the hospital, it had been pronounced cancer, but Emily had known better than that. Her mother had always been as healthy as an ox before Eddie had died. Her mother had died of a broken heart, unable to bear life anymore without her son after those two empty years. The second most terrible memory.

Emily had been twenty-five when her freshly twenty-year-old brother had died. She had been out of college for a couple of years. Then, when her mother had died, she had felt something snap in her brain. The thing that makes you get up in the morning when you don't want to, makes you stop at stop signs, or drive in a straight line down the road without zigzagging through the median. After that, she had decided to be in college again.

She would simply recreate the happiest times in her life, live them again. Live the times before Eddie had left her to go deer hunting that last time, leaving before she could even say goodbye besides cheerfully waving at them at a distance. Had she yelled out a goodbye to him or just waved? She could never remember that part right. It was as if there was a hole in her brain in that very spot and her memory always ran and jumped over it. Emily tried in vain to train her mind to go back to that dark, censored hole, peer in, and see what was lurking in there, but it never worked.

Sometimes in her nightmares, she saw herself screaming at Eddie Joe to not go into the woods, but in the nightmare she couldn't remember why exactly. It was just a terrible feeling and she couldn't explain it to him. He'd just laugh his big laugh at her and go on down the path. And, then she'd wake up and remember the reason, the way to convince him she wasn't crazy and that he had to stay at the house with her. But, then she was awake. She knew that it was too late to save him.

The dream had been every night there for several months and then slowly tapered off. Kenneth had helped to distract her, he was good at that. After making her decision to run away, she had easily hired someone to help fake her identity, taking her mother's maiden name of Jarvis – dropping the Hopkins for good, she wanted no connection to her father – and enrolling as an eighteen-year-old at age twenty-eight.

She could do it, too, with her looks. She had worked out daily, bought the best makeup. All the boys believed she was eighteen. All of the boys including one George Morris, an aspiring chemical engineer. He still believed he was three years her senior.

***

George swallowed heavily. His eyes were glazed over as Edmund talked and as he struggled to let it sink into his system that his entire adult life had been formulated from the base of a lie.

"So, the person that you met at the wedding had to be a friend of Emily's or something, to show you that she had family, in keeping with the story she'd told you earlier. Later, it must have just been convenient to put her made-up sister Cindy in London, where Marlena was in boarding school, so she could call freely without you suspecting her. Do you remember where Cindy started out being from?"

"She's always been in London."

"Makes sense. Marlena's been at the same school her whole life."

"I still can't believe that Emily had a child! This is… this is too much! Why didn't the lying minx even tell me that! A teenager, no less."

"She's thirteen."

"Have you met her, Edmund?"

"No, I haven't. I have wished to thousands of times, but I wouldn't know what I could or couldn't say to her without confusing the poor child. For all I know, Emily has lied to Marlena about me just like she lied to you."

Simon stood beside George but didn't speak, just awkwardly patted George's shoulder, his eyes wide. Simon puffed

Jessica D. Lovett

a breath onto his watch and polished it with the bottom of his tee shirt.

"My only grandchild…" Edmund trailed off, rubbing at his eyes.

"Simon?" George looked up at him.

"Yes?"

"I should have listened to you back in college."

The door swung open and Maddy came in. She walked straight to Simon and easily put her arms around him.

"Yes, you should have! I know how to pick women, case in point!" Simon laughed, smiling into Maddy's eyes.

Maddy batted her hand at Simon, flicking off the remark with her blithe expression.

"Whatever you're talking about, I probably don't agree. And, for that matter, you did not 'pick' me, I picked you. Case in point." Maddy lightly kissed his cheek.

"Nice to see you again," Edmund said.

"You, too, sir. George, how're you feeling?"

"Well, Miss Madeline, I'm ready. I remember the guy's name."

"Let's have it, George."

"He goes by Max. He's Max Blaine or Maxwell Blaine, or…"

Maddy's smile dropped off her face, every trace instantly gone as if it had never been there.

"What?" George stopped and stared.

"His name is Blaine Maxwell and I can't believe that he could possibly be the one who did this to you!"

"This is someone you associate with?" George said with such forcefulness that it caused his raw body to cough a little.

"Not really. Don't worry. He's a reporter at *The Times*. He has asked me out a couple of times, though."

Simon's hands formed a fist at his sides. George scowled.

"I'll bet he has. And, I hope you spat in his face," George muttered.

"I didn't say yes or anything. But, no spitting either. There always was something, something sort of off about him. Like he was less – or maybe more – than he seemed to be."

The men were silent.

"Don't worry, boys! I didn't know he was an evil bad guy, but I followed my feminine intuition and said no to the man. I was not a victim of his... his... ah..."

"Bad guy-ness," Simon finished.

"Precisely."

"But, I do know," Maddy added, "that he was sent to Mexico City to cover a story and I'll bet your Emily is with him."

"I'm impressed, Maddy. You're right up there with the police," Simon said as he fussed with her hair, Maddy gracefully moving his hand away and mouthing the word "later."

"Yeah, we knew it was Mexico. The cop told us. Yolanda sent out her entire network of friends and family over there to check all the sleazy motels in border towns for them already! She wanted to help George. I told her that that was crazy albeit sweet, but she insisted on emailing Emily's photo to them."

"She's a good lady."

"Yes, she is. She believes on taking, in her own words, plenty of shots in the dark."

***

Jessica D. Lovett

Something spindly and sharp poked at Emily's ear. Scratching it away, she awoke with a jolt. It was daylight. The light seemed to be causing pain around her eyes. Everywhere the light touched ached. The last thing she remembered was seeing Blaine's clenched teeth and feeling his hard breath against her chest as his muscular hands imprinted into her shoulders. They had pulled over after driving all day since early morning, surrounded by lonely fields with scattered blotches of yellow and blue wildflowers and tall, windswept grasses.

After jumping over the short barbed wire fence, they had watched dusk fade into night nestled in each other's arms. Carefree. Contented as she had been in who knows when, Emily had closed her eyes to the starry darkness around them and fallen asleep peacefully for what felt like an instant when she awoke and realized that she could not open them again.

The dark had settled in the creases in her eyelids, into every space where any light could creep in. Emily had begun to wonder if she had opened her eyes and the stars had all just disappeared or if her eyes were permanently shut. Everything felt so heavy. She didn't remember sleeping, but now, all of a sudden, it was morning. Dust was sticking to her sore inner thighs and she dashed it off.

Searching for her cell phone to check the time, she judged by the beating sun that if might even be early afternoon. After running her hands over the tops of the tall grasses and flowers, feeling around to find her panties and red tapered jeans, she dug her pink cell out of the slash pocket. 12:37pm.

Max must be off using a bush for a bathroom, she thought, though she couldn't see any bushes. There was no hiding behind the brushy mesquite trees around here. She fiddled with the rhinestone charms and beads hanging from her cell phone.

164

Emily's skin burned. When she moved and her skin shifted, it was as if flames were licking up upon her. Sitting up, she looked for the car to grab some lotion from her purse. Both shoulders of the highway were empty. Giving a one half of a second's thought to the idea that Max may've kindly gone out to get some food for them, Emily realized that, yes, she was alone. Again.

Max was gone. And, on top of that, he had taken her good Dooney and Bourke bag! It was probably already on a pawnshop's dusty shelf, she cursed under her breath. No cash, no luggage, but at least she had her half-charged phone, if it would even work out here in the dead center of nowhere. Emily started to stand but felt dizzy. Reaching up to steady herself, she felt a large knot on her head, half of the bruise peeking out from underneath her hairline.

"Max isn't very good at finishing the job, is he?" Emily whispered aloud to herself. Collapsing in a heap again after working so hard to get up, she mourned. How did anybody, anywhere ever know what love was? It always hides, is always disguised.

***

George tapped the table with his pen. Click, click, click. He clicked the point in and out, in and out, then started up tapping again. As if on cue, Simon got a pen from his pocket and started to tap on the floor in complimenting rhythms to George's taps, dragging and hitting out a primitive rock beat. George raised an eyebrow at him.

"Oh, yes, this is George Morris. It's fine. I didn't mind being on hold."

Jessica D. Lovett

"You did too mind!" Simon whispered loudly.

"Shhh, Simon!" George pushed the volume button on the phone.

"Yes, ma'am. I'd like to file an official, formal accusation. Indictment. Yes, that. Well, whatever it's called, I want to file one. Emily Jarvis Morris. Yes, she was. I mean, is. Technically still married, yes. Sorry." The next words came through George's clenched teeth, "Blaine Maxwell. Yes, I'm positive. I got the stitches to prove it."

chapter 15

BLAINE MAXWELL TURNED his cell phone on silent, ignoring the ten missed calls from Emily. What could he do now? He knew that he couldn't go back to Mexico City, act like nothing happened, and complete the story. Emily'd surely tell police that he had assaulted her and they would be all over him for that, given her forceful attitude and stunning looks, if they weren't already looking for him for the George thing.

"I wonder if the poor sap made it," Blaine chuckled to himself, passing a sun-bleached billboard advertising some hospital. The doctor and patient were shaking hands and grinning at the camera. Who needs an ad for a hospital, he thought. People just take you there when you have to go, to the nearest one you can get to, and nobody's smiling.

It was hard for Blaine to understand Dr. George Morris. Married to a beautiful woman, big fancy house, steady job that paid tons more than reporting news did, plus it was something respectable. Blaine had a cubicle, not an office with a plaque on the door with his name followed by abbreviated titles. What did George have to be unhappy about? George could have tried to make Emily happy, couldn't he? Tried to be the suave male type he knew that she wanted?

Yet, who was he kidding. Nobody could make that woman happy. She had no clue that what she really needed was a swift kick in the pants. *The real reason she took after me*, he mused, *was that I showed her who was boss.* George tried to give her what she wanted, give Emily all the silly things she asked for to appease her every-growing lust for life and yet that kind of generosity wouldn't help anything.

At this, Blaine pictured natives drumming harsh cadences as they stood beneath a giant golden statue version of Emily, as beautiful as ever, hands outstretched as George alone heaped wood on the fires of her bronze alter and brought more and more offerings to her feet. Her fire consumed it all into ash instantaneously, George running off into the forest to chop down more trees.

***

As Emily stared into the empty sky, leaning on the shaky support of a mesquite, she thought of Marlena. She laughed to herself, remembering the time that she had been talking on the phone to Marlena as she walked down the dorm hall after her gym class. Marlena had seen a poster of Calvin Elliot and a couple of other NFL players posing shirtless on a poster on the wall of an open dorm room. American football was all the rage at Marlena's school that year.

Completely clueless to the fact that Calvin was her father, Marlena had casually commented to her mother that that Calvin dude was "really hot for a football player." Emily had tried to hide her awkwardness, tried not to betray anything in her voice, only answering, "Why, yes, he is sweetie. He is that."

Just then, Emily could see a car in the distance. She jumped up, forgetting the dizziness she felt from sun sickness and her injury, and fell right down again, like a toddler first learning to walk. Rising up much more slowly, Emily began to wave her arms up in the air, wildly with her biggest grin, until she saw that the lights on the top of the vehicle. The car drove right up beside her and the cowboy hat wearing cop lowered his passenger side window, tipped his hat to her, and asked what he could do to help. As he helped her into the seat, as polite as anyone could be, Emily saw a photocopied print of her and Max's photos taped to the cop's dashboard. When he saw that Emily had seen them, he smiled.

"Yep. Now, don't you worry, ma'am. We'll treat you right fair as we can."

"But wait! I'm in Mexico! You can't do anything to me, cowboy! I'm…."

"Beg your pardon, ma'am, but actually you're about five miles outta Mexico. My jurisdiction."

Max. He did this on purpose, Emily raged, crossing her arms tightly in front of her. I'll get him back for this, she thought. But, then, what could she really do? Emily gnawed on these thoughts until they pulled up to the adobe style police station.

***

George's eyes began to flutter open. He had no idea how long he had been sleeping, but, looking over in the direction of his corner window and seeing Agnes there made him feel secure.

"Oh, did I wake you?"

"No."

Jessica D. Lovett

"Well, good. I mean, it's good you are awake, anyway. There's something you'll want to know that wasn't a good enough reason to wake you up for, but still, and..."

"Get on with it, Agnes. Nothing could surprise me at this point."

"They – the police – found her."

"Where?"

"She's in a hotel in Laredo – that's in Texas – being guarded by the police. She won't tell them anything."

George sighed and pulled his blanket over his head in dismay.

"She may've even had a touch of sunstroke. Sunburned badly, a blow on the head, stranded by the road..."

He pulled it down again, curious. As he was waking up, it had occurred to George that maybe Emily had fought against having children in order to cover up her lies to him about her age. After all, since Emily was thirty-two when they got married and not the twenty-two he believed her to be, and they had waited several years before he had brought up the idea of having children, she had just been past the medically recommended baby-bearing age. Maybe she wasn't all bad. Maybe she was really looking out, in a way, for the best thing for a baby. Maybe she didn't really despise kids, as she had claimed to, but had just known that it wouldn't have worked for her to try and be a mother. *What a pathetic attempt at logic*, he chided himself.

"At least she's away from that brute," he whispered.

Tears formed in the corners of George's eyes and he pulled the blanket up higher to camouflage them, quickly dabbing them off of his eyes. Without saying anything, Agnes grabbed George up and gave him a large – yet gentle, due to all his injuries – hug.

170

***

Simon and Maddy, Edmund, and Agnes had all come over to George's for supper. They had all chipped in for takeout. No one wanted to cook and no one felt like being alone, either. Simon secretly wished that they could've gotten pizza or Chinese or something less boring than plain roast chicken and vegetables, but that was what Maddy had requested so he had eagerly agreed.

"Some makeshift family this is turning out to be," Simon teased.

"And another thing," Agnes touched the table lightly with her tight fist, "since Emily's the only legal guardian of Marlena – Calvin having no rights at all – and Emily's being charged with felonies, doesn't that make Marlena up for adoption? Having just turned, what?"

"Thirteen," Edmund added.

"I will adopt her," George stated. It was a firm and plainly stated sentence. George sat unmoving in his wheelchair, looking like he was primed and ready to defend himself against anyone who wanted to tell him that adopting Marlena was a silly idea. No one did.

"Now. I will adopt Marlena now."

"What in the world will Emily say?" Agnes gasped.

"I don't care. Our lawyers are now *my* lawyers. Anyone that she can dig up to defend her pitiful case is bound to be less adequate than this firm that I've been with for years. They will fight for me. And, Emily will know that she owes this to me. She can pay me back for all the mess that she's made of my life by letting me get to know the daughter who I should have been allowed to adopt as a toddler in the first place."

"What if she's too stupid to know that she owes you?" Simon asked.

"Well, then, she'll give me the rights anyway. By force."

"What if she is unreasonable, as she has always proven herself to be?" Agnes blurted.

"If she's difficult, I won't sign the divorce papers and she'll be stuck with me. There's no way she'd allow that to happen. I have a feeling that Emily's freedom means more to her than the daughter she's stashed in London all this time."

"Wait, wait, wait! What about Edmund, here?" Agnes asked, taking Edmund's arm and raising it up into the air like they were taking role in class and she was making sure they saw that he was not absent.

"As I've already explained to George," Edmund added, looking down, "I can't adopt Marlena. Some part of me would like to, to know my... my only grandchild better, but I am just not in the best of... ah... positions to do so."

"What are you aiming at?" Agnes wove her eyebrows higher at each of Edmund's brief hesitations.

"Well, Agnes, you see... I took the so-called 'Ghandi prescription' from Chemi-Life for the better part of last year."

"No!"

"Yes. Though it didn't kill me within a month of taking it, like some of those other unfortunate folks, it has made me incapable of taking care of someone else. They don't know how long I can make it with the internal damage that the pill caused."

"Edmund! That's terrible," Agnes clasped her hands.

"Oh, don't fret about me, Agnes. I just wouldn't feel comfortable being responsible for someone else like that, especially someone like Marlena who has been through such pain, just to up and leave her without warning and cause her more pain."

"I see…" Agnes trailed off, wiping her eyes subtly with the sleeve of her cardigan. George nodded slowly, already in on this problem.

"That's part of why I wanted to make up with Emily. I wanted to see eye to eye with her before I lost my chance. Also, I wanted to give her the opportunity to apologize so that she wouldn't have it hanging over her heart when she found out I was gone. That is, if she were ever planning to apologize to me."

"She's sorry for abandoning her family like that, Edmund. Somewhere deep inside her soul she is," Agnes added, fervently

"If she has a soul," Simon muttered. Maddy elbowed him.

"You'll be the greatest dad ever, George," Maddy teased as she passed George the carrots.

"What a twisted loop the Chemi-Life creation has made around Edmund," George pondered to Simon when everyone else was in the kitchen grabbing a bite.

"Probably the 'religion pill' initially compelled Edmund to seek out his estranged daughter in the first place and then coldly shortened his lifespan so he couldn't take advantage of the emotional freedom he fought so hard for… with Emily or Marlena…"

"That sounds dramatic, George, but what makes you think that Emily would ever forgive him anyway? It's not as if she took that pill, too…"

***

Everyone else had left and Simon had just kissed Maddy goodbye, waving as her headlights traced the curvy driveway behind George's house. Simon leaned against the doorframe, absentmindedly watching until the very last dot of yellow headlight beam from her car had vanished into the night. George saw

Simon steal a glance at his watch, so he asked him the time. 9:24pm. A good enough time as ever to call the police about Chemi-Life's involvement in the deaths of all those innocent people for the sake of making a profit. Chemi-Life did not seem to indicate that they were slowing down production and that had been the last straw for George.

Yes, he would undoubtedly lose his job. There was no way to hide that he was the one who turned them in. Even if the police did try and protect him, who else had such information? Who else, besides him, would be willing to give it? Yes, they would probably blackball him, no matter what a judge ruled, just because the Chemi-Life higher-ups had friends in every corner. Yet, who cares? He couldn't sleep at night anymore – and if he did ever manage to drift into a weak sleep, he couldn't bear such slashing nightmares anymore – being on the payroll of a murderous company... even if he didn't have a hand in the actual deed.

***

Blaine felt like he was leading himself to the gallows, driving to Mexico City to cover the treaty story he'd been assigned by *The Times*, but he just didn't see any other option. He couldn't simply run away to Rio or somewhere... no cash. Blaine had been counting on Emily's greed to solve that problem, but someone had been smart and frozen George's accounts before they could get to it.

He would have plenty of opportunity to meet some friends and mold an alibi for the Emily thing later. He was good at that. Good at convincing people to lie for him. Blaine prided himself on his charisma and, most importantly, his innocent-looking apple pie face.

As for George's case, it was really George's word against his own, wasn't it? He would admit to having a brief affair with Mrs. Morris, but, who would put him in jail for that? Obviously, George would want to blame his wife's lover for the assault. Blaine would simply claim that the affair had been over long ago — if wouldn't matter if Emily protested to that. That would be a natural thing for a woman to do.

***

Janie affixed the carry-on tag to the well-loved red umbrella stroller and grabbed up her giggling toddler, by the hand. He clutched a patchwork teddy bear tightly in his other fist. The two older children, a boy and girl with matching light complexions and golden hair, joined hands with their mother and brother and they made a train of four into the oval door of the passenger plane. The oldest boy, a bright child of six-and-a-half noticed the other passengers struggling through the tight aisles with their carry-on bags.

"Why don't we have suitcases, Mama?" He nervously pulled his hands away and stuck them into his jean jacket pockets.

"Yeah, and why isn't Daddy coming with us?" whined his four-year-old sister. Janie was hoping that the details would elude her children. There was nothing she could do but tell the truth to them, she rationalized. Even being young, they deserve the truth.

So much of Janie's life for almost the past decade had been based on lies... lie after lie from Peter that he would not seduce

Jessica D. Lovett

his patients. Lie upon lie that he loved her. That he loved his children. The last words she, hopefully, ever heard come from his perfect lips were even lies... "If you just give me another chance, Janie, I'll be true to you, I will! I will change!" She would forever hear him whispering those words to her on the phone, trying desperately for the coworkers around him to not hear the distress in his voice and pry.

"Well, darlings, we don't have suitcases because we were in a hurry and we are going on an adventure! We are going to have a new life together! We are going to New York to stay with Grandma Agnes for a while... You know you all love her so much. Won't that be fun?"

"What about Daddy?"

"Well, he...ah... he decided not to come."

"But, Mommy, if we don't have a suitcase what'll we do?"

"We will simply get new everything... new pajamas, new toothbrushes, new everything... How's that?"

"Do I get to pick what color? Last time we got toothbrushes I didn't get to pick and I don't like purple."

"Any color you like, baby, any color you like."

***

Music was blaring on Blaine's state-of-the-art stereo system. He was having the time of his life. Such freedom he had never tasted. The rental place had even happened to a bright yellow convertible in stock... It was truly his lucky day. He didn't notice any other headlights near him on the dark road and wondered if maybe he had left a stray french fry or two in his fast food sack wadded up on the floor of the passenger seat.

Lunging over, he groped around with his right hand... Where was that thing? Just a second... Almost... got it! Grabbing the grease-soaked sack, he fretted over his decision to sully the car's interior with it. Was there a fee for that? If you made a mess in the rental car? Probably not. It cost him enough. Did any ketchup leak? Where was a napkin... There's one around here, somewhere...

Blaine propped the wheel up on his left knee as he bent in half to reach the small stack of clean napkins just below the passenger seat. Blaine anticipated and felt nothing as the driver of an eighteen-wheeler, drunk with lack of sleep, whipped the tiny sports car into a sphere of solid yellow in a matter of choppy instants, like one might mindlessly whisk the yolk of an egg.

chapter 16

MARLENA SAT ON the plane, awkwardly thumbing through a book she'd already finished hours ago. It had been hard to leave the energy and electricity of London behind. It was home. Watching familiar buildings and landmarks fade into clouds had almost made her cry but not quite. It was probably not goodbye forever, right? She had no idea what was in store.

Left alone to her thoughts, she was ushered back in her mind to one of the last conversations she had had with her mother before all this craziness had happened. Well, before she was aware that it was happening. Marlena had considered trying out for the freshman cheerleading squad at her school the next semester and her mom had kind of flipped out about it. Her mom usually didn't boss her around about anything, but this time she really had let Marlena have it... the only big speech about life and all that kind of stuff that she remembered her mom ever giving her.

"You know what being a cheerleader – the head cheerleader – in high school taught me, Marlena?"

"Wow, Mom, I didn't know you were a cheerleader, anyway, but I guess it taught you how to do cool flips and stuff!"

"No. Well, yes. That. But I mean that it taught me to yell at boys, at men, yell at them as loud as I could... physically

Jessica D. Lovett

YELL at their ears and their eyes 'til I was the one they noticed. The one that stood out. The one they wanted."

"Oh. I... uh...." Marlena couldn't repond, but it didn't matter, since her mom wasn't done and the words couldn't be stopped now. She hated when her mom tried to talk about the "birds and the bees" with her. She wasn't stupid. She knew where babies came from. Sometimes her mom forgot she was thirteen!

"Pretty soon I began to forget what my real voice sounded like in all the yelling. Then I liked the Yelling Emily better than my old voice. Yelling wins. You've got it figured out, Marlena, be glad you're not pretty."

"Well, thanks a lot, Mom!" Marlena shoveled as much sarcasm onto her words as she could to bury the hurt.

"No, I mean that in a good way, promise."

"Uh huh..."

"Being pretty is miserable. Never try to be pretty. No one will really love you unless you yell, yell louder than all the other pretty people yelling. Be a real person. Just be you."

"I'll do my best to be as ugly as possible, Mom!"

Marlena was yelling. She didn't mean to. All this talk about yelling. She hoped her mom couldn't tell through the phone.

"No, baby, I always mess stuff up. That's not what I mean. You are a beautiful person, Marlena Jarvis. You still have a soul in you."

"Thanks. I guess."

"When Eddie Joe was killed so... so... terribly, I didn't want to remember my old voice ever, ever again. I killed it, too, because when I heard it, I thought of him. That's the reason, I guess. Yes, that's the reason."

180

"Mom, I'm sorry..."

"Balancing on some hot guy's shoulders was easy, but I never could figure out how to stand up by myself."

It was weird hearing her mom say a guy was "hot" and she still had no idea exactly what her mom meant by all that. Marlena did not try out for cheerleading, at any rate. She joined chess club instead. She hoped that her mom would be happy with that.

The pilot's voice boomed over the speakers for them to buckle up but she didn't hear him. The sudden loud chorus of seat belt clickings were what had jolted her out of her reverie. She hoped that someone would tell her what was going on soon. She didn't want to miss the chess tournament next Thursday.

***

No one came into her hotel room that night. When the hospital had released Emily, the cowboy cop had shown pity to her and put her up in a motel behind the police station – under lock and key, of course. There was – or so they told her – a officer outside the door. Emily had left a note, in case someone should come. The note was beside her cell phone, backlight asleep, but with her contacts open to Marlena should one click the "home" button. The note read:

> *Three things. Please tell Marlena Jarvis that her father is Calvin Elliot the football player and that her real daddy is Dr. George Morris and that I should have let him be her daddy all along. Tell her I'm sorry.*
>
> *Tell Edmund Jarvis I forgive him.*

Jessica D. Lovett

>*Tell Dr. George Morris I am sorry for making him marry me and sorry for everything after that.*
>
>*Make that four things. Somebody find Blaine Maxwell who writes for the paper in NYC and tell him what happened to me so he'll feel like a jerk for leaving me like that.*

In her flawlessly manicured hand was an empty bottle of antidepressants, manufactured by Chemi-Life and a bottle of the trendiest, designer bottled water was turned on its side and slowly trailing out from just under the bedskirt, making a carpeted puddle around her equally flawlessly manicured feet.

Emily made no attempt to stop the water from chugging out and soaking into the carpet. No need to. She planned to never clean up another mess she'd made again. *Twenty pills oughta do it*, she mused, *twenty-something was about all that was left.* In the cavernous silence, she waited.

***

Marlena flinched. The word "adoption" had been thrown into Mrs. Westley's phone conversation with someone… someone Marlena clearly didn't know. That was the last time she'd heard her stoic but beloved advisor's voice. Would it be truly the last time? Mrs. Westley had said "adoption" with a sort of an up-turned note of a question at the end of it, stopping short when she saw Marlena's eyes alight in shock, bringing the hushed conversation back into loud reality. Marlena had also overheard the name "George" before the conversation had been clipped short.

Was this George guy a boyfriend of her mother's? Was her mother finally going to find a nice man and settle down and be happy? Give Marlena a normal family? A dad? A real home? Or... Was...

"Mrs. Westley! Did my mom...? Is she...? Is she alive? Is she okay?"

Mrs. Westley had been quick to banish Marlena's fears with plenty of uncharacteristic warm hugs and repeated-too-many-times phrases like, "No, dear, no... Nothing like that..." and "Don't you worry, dear, it'll all be alright."

Usually when people used those phrases in the movies it meant that things were not in deed going to be alright, but Marlena had tried to shovel her trust into Mrs. Westley's words. Mrs. Westley had never lied to her before. Surely there was no reason for her to start now.

Mrs. Westley had told her that it wasn't her place to tell Marlena all the details, that she'd leave that to Marlena's family, but that Marlena was to get on a plane alone and go to New York City to meet George, whoever he is. Since her mom wasn't dead, Marlena figured that the first scenario was correct and that he must be a boyfriend or fiancé or something. Weird that her mom never mentioned being serious about someone like that.

Then again, Marlena thought, her mom never really was too upfront about private things in her life with her. Marlena hated being treated like a shielded little child. But, sometimes, shields are nice, she had realized several hours ago, as she'd walked alone to board a huge plane filled to the brim with strangers...

***

George watched as the red and blue racing stripe of the passenger jet plane slowly trailed along and then stopped still. The heat from the engines made the air around the plane shimmer.

First wiping his nervous palms on his jeans, George gripped the arm rests of his wheelchair until the metal underneath the thin foam padding made indentions on his fingers.

"Perfectly on time," Simon said, looking at his watch and patting George on the back.

"Time's actually on my side, today, eh?" George smiled.

George had no trouble spotting Marlena in the stream of exiting passengers. When he saw a younger, quite lanky version of the Emily he had first met walk off of the plane and catch their eyes, smiling awkwardly, he knew that he had won. He was starting over, living a new, real life and no one could ever take it from him again. He refused to be alone in his spirit.

"Hey, there! I'm Marlena!" a shinier, more chipper version of Emily's voice said to them, partly yelling over the bustling crowds.

"Hello! I guess you know I'm George Morris and this is my friend slash temporary wheelchair-pusher, Simon Kincade."

Marlena vigorously shook their hands as various key fobs on her rainbow colored messenger bag jangled in time with their exchanges. Marlena looked around for, presumably Emily, which would be a natural thing to do, George thought. He begged her silently in his mind not to ask where Emily was.

Marlena took over pushing George's wheelchair and Simon took Marlena's one suitcase.

"Need to pick up any more luggage, Marlena?" Simon asked, as they passed the crowed baggage claim area.

"Nope, I'm a light traveler."

There was silence for a few moments. Not like her mother at all so far, George mused. Suddenly Marlena stopped pushing the wheelchair and George could feel his muscles all tense, waiting for the underlying question... *Where is my mother?* He wanted to close his eyes and retreat into his chair like he was a tortoise and it was his strong shell.

"I want to say something."

"Go ahead, kid."

"Ummm... Thank you for wanting me. Wanting to adopt me and all. No one else ever has."

Tears welled up in George's eyes again as this bright-eyed sprite of a person actually thanked him for offering to adopt her. It wasn't official yet, but they would at least have a trial run of it and see how they got along. And, how had she known about that part in the first place? Mrs. Westley was supposed to have been tight-lipped about the whole thing. What exactly did Marlena know about the whole situation and what was his job to tell her?

"How about let's go home?" George offered.

"Sure, let's go home."

JESSICA D. LOVETT is an author and avid reader, who has long been passionate about writing books for both adults and children. She is also a musician who plays the guitar, piano, and flute. She holds a master's degree in humanities with an emphasis in creative writing from Tiffin University and a bachelor of arts degree in literature from Howard Payne University. Currently, the author and her husband are building a fledgling homestead with their two young children which hosts a gigantic white dog, a growing flock of Easter Egg chickens, and a chicken-herding cat. *Transplanting Hope* is her first novel. Her website is jessicadlovett.com.

17720512R00117

An aspiring mystery writer mines his world for greater meaning, and perhaps a soul mate along the way. A kind-hearted chemical engineer casts a cold eye on his disappointing marriage. A stunning journalist conceals her surprising shyness through her well-chosen words. *Transplanting Hope*, the debut work of fiction by Jessica D. Lovett charts the sometimes hapless, sometimes hopeful lives of divergent individuals whose paths cross in the heat of a corporate cover up, and whose connections help each of them heal past wounds and find inroads to heartening new horizons.

Being born with a silver spoon, the happy-go-lucky novelist Simon Kincade has the luxury to dabble in mysteries with his poison pen, while living in considerable comfort. His best friend from college, Dr. George Morris, faces an altogether different reality each day. His job at the pharmaceutical company Chemi-Life is proving complex, and his marriage to the shopaholic Emily has long since soured. Simultaneously, *Times* reporter Madeline Bryson learns her job is on the line. Her hunt for a job-saving story entwines all of them in a sinister swirl that exposes far more than any of them had bargained for. As old secrets are unearthed and new allegiances are fused, *Transplanting Hope* offers a richly drawn, suspenseful foray into three lives, and how feelings, failings, hearts, and hopes can be transformed by chance meetings and redemptive twists of fate. Intimate and optimistic, this deeply affecting novel offers a richly drawn look at the human experience, one individual at a time.

ISBN 978-1481988216

9 781481 988216

Cover photo
©Darroll G. Wright, 2012

eLeCTRiC
miRaGe
PUBLISHING CO.